SECOND CHANCE *in* TANGIER

A Novel

ANOUAR MAJID

Published by
Tingis Books
tingisbooks.com

A Project of Tingis Magazine
Founded in 2003
tingismagazine.com

First paperback edition

ISBN: 978-0-578-70895-9

CAFE SMARA

There is no telling what the man might be thinking. He sat precariously against the wall of Cafe Smara, as Ashab's Cafe came to be known since the death of its creative founder, facing rows of men watching two Casablanca soccer teams fight it out on the screen. My father had told me that in his youth Lamin Majriti would have never spent any time watching Moroccan soccer games on television. Real soccer passions were reserved for select European teams, not wasted on low-level games such as these. Tangier had its own squad now in the premier league and that, too, must have been a novelty for Lamin who had once written a story about a soccer player from another time, the now-forgotten Si Yussef Khaldi.

It was, actually, disconcerting, if not quite painful, to see Lamin as if he were trapped in a bus looking sideways at passengers, while the men and two women who were engrossed in the soccer game were totally unaware of his presence. Mohamed, the waiter who had replaced his legendary namesake M'hammed, and Si Merzouk, the new owner, were trying to make their new-old customer comfortable, even if he tried hard to persuade them to let him be and not make a fuss about his needs. Was Lamin really looking at the people as he seemed to be? Or was he merely looking through them, to times, histories, and futures, vanished and yet to come? A quick glance and I thought of time suspended, in limbo, as if the speed of globalization were too fast for flesh-and-blood human beings designed, at best, for the rhythms of the Stone Age. What was Lamin looking at? Where was he? Where?

The only place I could find when I walked into the cafe that Sunday afternoon was a seat against the opposing wall—which was a window giving out onto the terrace with its giant plant pots shielding the customers—putting me in a perpendicular line of vision and allowing me to scrutinize the man undetected. As the customers made their usual soccer outbursts in support of this or that team, I scanned the milieu to understand why, in this city of a million cafes, Lamin chose to spend his time in one that had lost its luster and even its own prized gadget—the blender. I was actually seized by a sense of shock when the waiter told me juices were now made in the *malbana*—I guess you'd call that a dairy store— next door, sitting next to glasses and various cheeses, including the local feta variety, ready to turn into action. I figured that what with all the diet fads, gradual spread of herbalists, the growing mania for physical fitness, the tell-all talk shows that every cab driver in the city had on the radio, as if the whole city on wheels was listening to its dark side and emerging out of the taxi, after paying five or ten dirhams, to bask into the sunlight of renewal and walk unknowingly, confidently, toward a future that keeps stretching away forever, even leaping over the crisp outline of Spain, just fourteen kilometers beyond the horizon, to agricultural fields in some Spanish province, and beyond that to the streets of Barcelona, then further up to the gray urban areas of France, Belgium and

Holland, until they vanish entirely northwards, making their way to the forbidding climes of the Arctic and simply falling off the face of the earth.

In Tangier, things are never what they seem to be and one thing leads to another and then another until we find ourselves back where we started.

Lamin didn't have to be in this cafe, no matter the memories. It felt like an offense, as if he had chosen to spend his time in hostile territory, exposing his delicate sensibilities to a crowd of rough men who, I can bet anyone, had never read a single book, and spent their time arguing over soccer teams and watching a never-ending series of games made available daily, almost twenty-four seven, through satellite TV and the ubiquitous BEIN channel, the Qatari sister to Al Jazeera that covered sports events in many languages around the world. When I think about it now, I marvel at how a tiny country, smaller than the province that includes Tangier, has managed to spread its addictive brew of breaking political news and heart-stopping sports duels to remove a huge swath of the Arab male species from any meaningful productive life and glue them to super-wide LG screens attached to any wall space cafes could afford. And then the same Arab men, when they had a moment between games, would make the only statement that made them seem interested in culture, and that is the old, very old refrain of "Our world is not what it used to be," as if things had gone gradually worse since Muslims lost the golden age of Al-Andalus, the glittering civilization of philosophy, poetry, and science that flourished, right there, across the sea, in Spain. Then it was back to reality and a soccer fest that was programmed to last till the end of times.

I know that in Tangier writers and cafes are an inextricable part of the same mythos, but I can't think of a writer or thinker who has been associated with this kind of cafe, certainly not someone like Lamin and who had spent his time thinking about the deep ravine that separates East from West, impatiently weaving ropes that might allow the brave to make it to one side or another, sitting stoically in a cafe whose name few in the city of Tangier know. I definitely couldn't see him on the second floor battling rivals in never-ending parcheesi games. This was no Cafe de Paris, Cafe Baba or Cafe Hafa. This was no Bar Negresco, either, the place once frequented by the city's iconoclastic rebel, Mohamed Choukri, the autodidact who managed to dazzle the world with his literary erudition, steadfast courage, and routines of dissipation until he reached the pantheon that only the traveler Ibn Batouta had occupied. Choukri was proof that one doesn't have to go to China, as the prophetic tradition would have it, to acquire knowledge. Living in Tangier was enough to open vast worlds of possibility before the habitual *sharqi*, the furious easterly wind that drives Tangerians gradually insane, blow by blow, as if the bloody east, where fire-and-steel religions were forged, had vowed to punish a city that chose to do things its own way. Even today, this metropolitan powerhouse, with its high rises, underpasses, broad avenues, underground parking, major ports, and, thanks to the tireless work of my own father, the magical Al Boraq, the train that gets you to Casablanca in less than two hours and a half, the city feels like a dream, as if it were temporarily stationed in this part of the world before making its way to some other place. It was hard to shake this feeling of being somewhat in waiting mode, as if Tangier were supposed to have been established somewhere else, maybe in Spain, or Italy, or, perhaps, Mexico. Or, perhaps, now that I think of it, she is what remains of the buried

Atlantis, built on what debris bubbled up to the top of the ocean and hastily attached itself to this corner of the African continent as a stepping point to some other world. But here she stayed, like an illegal immigrant in limbo, waiting for new directions that have yet to come.

My excitement was coursing through my body like wildfire as I pondered these issues, as if I were about to enter Atlantis itself and decipher for myself, once and for all, the elusive spirit of the city that has consumed Lamin's attention all his life and that is now haunting me in turn. I scanned the cafe looking hard for people who might have an idea about Lamin's long-ago acquaintance with Si Yussef. Except for Mohamed the waiter and no more than a handful of men well past their sixties, I could see no one. For a man who had traveled so widely and so regularly around the globe, the few trophies, including a faux world cup and a Moroccan flag that sat on top of a four-tiered glass cabinet with different breads, croissants, biscuits, Nutella, honey, Nescafé, Cola Cao, and Laughing Cow cheeses were certainly not the main attractions. The No Smoking and WiFi signs were plausible reasons, but that just wasn't convincing to me. In this setting, Lamin looked too regular, too nondescript to be of any significance. Yet here I was making a life-changing decision to write about him, as if he were some big political figure, a retired general who led wars, or a famous soccer player who fell on hard times. I was delaying my Ph.D. education to understand a man about whom I had heard about all my life. It's as if the figure of Lamin beckoned to me from across the ocean and lured me back to a self I was fast forfeiting in the streets of New York City. To justify my decision, I convinced myself that I'd write a book, but what kind of book, what genre, what style, and for which audience I had not the slightest clue. At the very least, a record of my attempt would survive and, at best, I would gain a new knowledge, perhaps a new consciousness to sustain me in hard times. It's as if knowing Lamin had become a condition sine qua non for my future plans, and that sealed my choice and removed any possibility of regret. The thrill of taking the risk of leaving my formal education behind for the sake of a story was too priceless to waste on the altar of certificates. If I could recalibrate my vision after talking to the man, I would consider myself successful, ready to take on the world and build a life on solid foundations.

I had always wondered whether I chose to major in American literature and do a master's in the United States because of Lamin's subtle influence. At first, I thought I was asserting my independence and doing my thing, rejecting the Moroccan filial obligation of following in my father's academic and professional footsteps. Then, realizing that this sort of rebellion is unwarranted, given the love, affection, and support my parents had given me, I tried to convince myself that I chose the literary path because I suspected that my father, a precocious boy of his generation in Tangier's public-school system, had no option but to choose a career in engineering, even though he cherished Sufi chants and classical poetry. Engineering, to me, was a military discipline, requiring boots on the ground, and that was not, by any stretch of imagination, how I saw my sweet-soul father. It definitely was not for me. Only later, when I was doing my graduate work at New York University, did I realize that I may have been influenced by my father's childhood friend. At first, I chased the thought away with a quick contortion of my face, but Lamin's published account of the Tangerian soccer player stuck in my mind and would simply not let go of me. In any case, the more I thought about my somewhat reckless decision to abandon my doctoral program, the more I realized that I had no choice in the matter. Lamin would later tell me that it is futile to try to make sense of or resist the eccentric impulses that seize Tangerians and that it would be best to let oneself go and hope for smooth sailing and safe landing. Returning to Tangier to write the story of Lamin was not a huge risk, anyway—I was coming home, even though I grew up in Rabat. And I knew, just as Lamin had known, that the story would unfold other stories, and that Tangier's record will be kept despite the proliferation of travel guides, online reviews, twenty-four-hour channels, and the endless noise of gadgets. Someone had to keep writing the story of a city that American expatriates had no clue about, the place without cocktail parties or hashish tales, just people speaking *darija*, the only dialect that captures the Moroccan soul, and trying to raise, feed, and, at best, educate their children. And when these *darija*-speaking people abandon themselves to nightlife, the pleasures are multiplied, leaving the non-*darija*-speaking strangers standing cold and smiling blandly, helplessly disconnected from the joy of locals and finding solace in the fact they are foreign. The tomes they had read while doing reconnaissance on the country they decided to seek shelter in told them nothing about Morocco's spirit that could only be conveyed in the *darija* and nothing else.

These were most unformulated thoughts in my head as I struggled to understand my decision to move to New York and pursue an education that would land me no job. But it was in a New York library that I discovered Lamin's account of Si Yussef and my father's native city, and that was enough to justify my two years of subway riding and endless quests for meaning in a city and country where ideas and recipes are like disposable fashion items, consumed today and discarded tomorrow, as if the world can't stand a recipe, book, film, or idea to last for a year, let alone ten, not to mention a century. Watching people on impossible quests for some kind of sexual utopia or a meaningful life was getting old. Two years were enough to give me pause and make me reconsider before I embark on longer journeys and find myself entangled in a permanent relationship or a career and saddling myself with chains too thick to break.

Finding Lamin was a moment of truth for me, a turning point. I got up from my table and walked in his direction, now that the cafe was mostly empty and the men and two women who had covered every inch of its bus-like space had suddenly left it deserted. I tried to look casual, as if I were just coming to say hello, as if I hadn't taken a leap of faith and traveled from New York just to talk to him. He was still looking sideways, this time not at the people watching television, but at the cafe's window that looks out onto the potted terrace and, behind it, the chairs lined up against the wall of Souk Mhadj El Kbir, the flower-and-pet market that also sold fresh fruit, produce and live chicken. It was in this market, during its heyday, when every stall was teeming with rich, colorful produce, that Lamin's neighborhood friend known as Cabeza because he got a kick out of big or misshapen heads met the Frenchwoman who gave him his first full-time job. Cabeza used to carry her heavy bags to her car, and one day she hired him to walk her dogs on the beach by her apartment near the port. In time, he took her dogs to her big mansion in Jbel Kbir, the leafy mountain on the hill overlooking the ocean and the neighborhood of Dradeb, and led a bucolic life with the dogs, among a strange group of mostly shabby Europeans who fancied themselves aristocrats on the Jbel. It was in this house that Lamin spent many days studying for his exams when he was in high school and when he was back from the university in Fez. Lamin could tell that Cabeza got some pleasure out of this because his friend never got beyond the first grade, having failed two years in a row and was promptly kicked out. His life circumstances, Lamin knew, were not optimal for him to get beyond this first academic hurdle. Still, Cabeza found some success as an insurance salesman and broker of all kinds of deals. He even ran for office twice, with different parties, including one whose name he couldn't remember. Who says that democracy is only a Western affair?

Just as I got closer to Lamin, he turned abruptly and almost immobilized me with his soft and otherworldly gaze. Then he spoke as if we had been in continuous contact, as if I hadn't been out of his sight since the few occasions we met in the company of my father or my entire family.

"Ahlan," he started. "How's your father? The family?"

"All good, Si Lamin."

"And America?"

"Good, too."

"Your studies?"

"I got my master's. I wrote my thesis on William Faulkner."

"Faulkner? Does anybody care about him anymore? That's some courage."

"Thank you. I know you liked him, so I got interested in him. Hard to read, but the substance is the stuff of life itself."

"Remind me how old you are. Twenty-five?"

"Exactly, Si Lamin."

"That's a great age. A quarter of a century. When the

senses are half-baked. It's one of the main crossroads of life. Any plans for the future? A Ph.D. perhaps?"

I paused, hesitating, wondering, fearing to say the wrong thing and provoke a contretemps that would derail my enterprise. He looked at me steadily, waiting for an answer.

"Not yet. I am postponing that project until I am ready."

"Ready for what?"

"I don't know. What kind of life I want to have. I don't know."

He pulled out a chair that seemed to have been stuck under the round table and invited me to sit. The waiter was now gone, walking around the terrace, catering to the many customers who had assembled to drink mint tea and café-au-lait. Suddenly, the space inside seemed eerily quiet, except for the humming of the television screen that had now switched to some nature program as if for a brief respite from enduring daylong soccer commentators putting viewers on edge with their dramatic blow-by-blow description of the action. I felt a thrill course through my body again, but I maintained my composure and kept a cool face, pretending that I was not Moroccan, but some kind of poker-faced, square-faced gringo. Lamin's glass of black light coffee was empty, with only a small cinnamon stick remaining inside. As I braved myself to face him without averting my look, or staring slightly past his right shoulder as I would have done, I looked him right in the eye to make sure I had the fortitude to engage him for whatever time we had. He seemed a bit younger than his age of almost sixty, but how much younger it was hard to tell. He'd always had wrinkles on his forehead and around his eyes, yet something about his expression suggested youthfulness. He was definitely a man still in his prime, yet his demeanor seemed to suggest that he was spent, as if he had lived three or four full lives and had decided that it was time to quit. He was neither too chubby nor properly slim, just the regular body of a middle-aged man who is not irreversibly old. His clothing suggested a downgrading of lifestyles and tastes, as if he had stepped away from a world of privilege into the humble routine of an average retiree overnight. He looked so nondescript that I wondered about my own sanity, afraid that I might have given up my life in New York to look for something in a man who was done thinking and writing and who was here for reasons too mundane to warrant my heroic action.

I asked him if he wanted anything to drink; he said no, but called the waiter and asked him to give me whatever I wanted. I requested mint tea with reduced sugar. I had discovered that in Morocco I can always alternate my caffeinated drinks between *café allongé* and mint tea, using the latter as a palate cleanser from the excessive bitterness that accumulates in my mouth over the course of the day.

"How's Tangier these days?" I started by asking innocuously.

"Healthy. Cleaner. More prosperous."

The crisp sunny air of that January seemed to confirm his opinion.

"It's obvious to anyone now. Especially in winter, when the city is less crowded. You can see how clean the streets are—as long as you don't look closely in untended green areas and parks."

"I know. Hard to change the habits of the souk. Maybe the new malls will help some. You can't have empty plastic bags and bottles on the floor of Zara."

I smiled. He knows Zara?

"That Ibn Batouta mall is quite good. Good coffee shop on top."

He didn't answer. I knew he came back to Tangier alone, leaving his wife and son behind.

"How do you find the social life here?"

"As good as it ever was. A bit too busy for my taste, but our culture endures. You just have to look a bit harder to find it. It's definitely there, everywhere."

I asked what he meant by culture and he simply said, "Spirit. Just spirit."

Mohamed served my tea. I took a sip. It was a bit sweeter than I had hoped, but that was to be expected because sweetness is relative here; it depends on luck, the insight of the waiter, and the skill of the tea maker behind the counter. In this case, it was Tefo, a waif of a man, with a stray mustache hanging down on both sides of his mouth, with one side longer than the other, as if the mustache was there not because Tefo wanted it but because the mustache made its own decision not to be shaved, forcing the man and his mustache to coexist in a sort of friendly truce. Tefo spent most of his day making coffee and tea, but his hands smelled exclusively of mint, whose fresh leaves he clipped to insert in tea pots or long glasses, like the one I had been served. How much sugar he put in each glass or tea pot depended on so many factors, including the last time he had had his smoke of *kif* on the roof of the cafe. Thus, one can't have the same glass of mint tea, with or without reduced sugar, in Cafe Smara, or Tangier, or any other place in Morocco because all measures are circumstantial.

I thought of my experiences back in New York, at Starbucks, or some other artisanal coffee shop, where great effort is made to offer authentic cafe experiences and how the whole thing looked so artificial when compared with the real thing in Tangier. Centuries of civilization, or lack thereof, separated Tefo from the young, university-educated baristas in American coffee houses. Unless one is talking about Dunkin Donuts—but that's a place I honestly don't know. I only had coffee there once and it tasted like fluoride with a faint taste of the coffee bean.

"This is the real cafe experience," I commented. "Drinking tea or coffee here is already a strong reminder that we are not in America."

"I agree," Lamin replied with a smile. "I have always thought that drinking coffee or tea is a great cultural ritual, one that seems to escape the eye of anthropologists and sociologists who are too busy with big ideas. An entire world is around us, right here, at this little table, but it requires knowledge and a keen eye to see. This is what real education does. It opens eyes."

Once again, an electrifying thrill coursed through my body, this time stronger than the last. I was almost propelled to stand up and shout "Yes!" but I forced myself to stay put and steady. In that moment, I knew I had made the right decision to come here, to meet this man, and try to write about him, and us, and you, too. This was enormous. These were the things that institutions don't see, money doesn't buy, and power can't get. This was freedom itself.

"I see, I see," I said, cheerfully, so as not to seem indifferent to his remarks. I didn't want my attempt at appearing cool to work against me. This was an initial encounter that I was trying hard to manage, almost as if I were giving birth to a new relationship, a new life.

"There is something formulaic about education these days. It's what people do, are expected to do. Who doesn't want to give an education to their children? It's like another activity that's for sale. The higher the price, the better the quality is supposed to be. Like buying a Mercedes or a BMW. Not the same as a Peugeot or a Renault."

"You are right. Education was once sacred, but the magic has been taken out of it. Did you say you wrote a thesis on Faulkner? Did I tell you that I refused to read American literature after Faulkner? OK, I must have read a couple of novels by contemporary writers, like Thomas Pynchon and Toni Morrison, but they felt contrived and uninspired, not anything like Faulkner's Columbian successor, Gabriel García Márquez. Modern American culture has stripped life of depth and tragedy and reduced everything to commercial transactions. And they think the Russians will get them! Maybe they should. The Russians still have soul—dark, maybe—but it's alive. Not deadened by anxiety, stress, debt, and wealth."

"Funny, I had an Iranian friend who once told me that his ideal day would consist of working in Connecticut and walking out to Teheran in the evening. American workplace efficiency and Iranian social and cultural life."

"Wish life was that simple. For me . . . "

He was interrupted by someone shouting his name from the door. "Lamin!"

We looked up to see a Spanish-looking man with a thick, leather coat and a tired smile.

"Lamin," he repeated. "I was hoping I'd see you. I heard you came here last Wednesday."

Lamin got up. "Hamid, is that you? What a great day!"

They walked toward each other and hugged in the middle of the narrow cafe, as Tefo, smiling to share in the joy of the moment, was stuffing yet another batch of mint leaves in a tea pot.

I could see the bonds that tied the two men right there, without having to find out, making Lamin's claim that events, by themselves, with no explanation, were enough to convey entire lifetimes, just as that hug did, and Hamid explaining casually that he was on his way upstairs to play parcheesi with his bitter rivals, and that he had been playing in the same spot for the previous twenty years, making it the one constant in his life besides banking, a profession he stumbled into after he had despaired of attaining a degree in economics while studying in Fez with Lamin. I could see the older Hamid and Lamin going all the way back to the legendary Ibn Al Khatib lycée, causing mischief everywhere, hanging out in cafes to watch soccer games, and playing on the beach, with Hamid being the goalkeeper of the team, smoking red Marlboros during the game, as if a goalie was half player and half spectator, doing what he can to stay entertained, especially during the winter months when the ocean winds of the Mediterranean grow chilly and damp. I could see the two friends riding a bus to Fez, and Lamin fumbling for his ID to show the police who had blocked the two-way road, Morocco's major highway at that time, and the police officer who was checking the passengers' IDs somehow miraculously overlooking Lamin, who had no ID on him and had already resigned himself to being pulled out of the bus and interrogated for hours. But it didn't happen, and Hamid was relieved for not losing his friend to the road and go all by himself to the ancient city of Fez. And there they were in Fez, both enrolling in economics before Lamin, at the last minute, and for some inexplicable reason, except perhaps in honor of his father, switched colleges and enrolled in English, attracted by the thrill of exoticism, English manners and American optimism to commit to a program that offered no financial rewards at the end. I could see the two young men sharing a dorm room, along with other friends from Tangier, eating in the cafeteria, and running away from the army that had invaded the campus in response to some violence that had erupted between Islamists and Communists, and Lamin and Hamid running into the wild open spaces beyond the campus, seeking refuge under the hot sun, before they could return to their rooms, retrieve their belongings, and leave the now-occupied campus until order would be restored and classes resumed.

"This is Rafik," Lamin introduced me. "Just came back from America."

"Oh, no! Another one crosses the Atlantic. It used to be Belgium. France. Holland, I don't know. But America? You started it," Hamid accused Lamin.

"Blame your father, Hamid. I consulted with him about leaving. Remember? You probably don't. Anyway, I was trying to decide between Europe and America and he was unequivocal: 'If you must go begging, knock at the door of the biggest house.' A mansion, I guess. That's what I did. I took a plane to New York, the biggest house of all."

Hamid didn't respond but kept his smile. Lamin added: "May he rest in peace."

As Hamid picked up his parcheesi table and walked upstairs to do battle, Lamin explained to me that Hamid's father had been a high-level functionary in the local tax office and that he had taught his son to play not soccer, the popular sport, but handball, a sport that is virtually unknown in America. It is for that reason that he was chosen to be the goalie of his team and do what he could to keep his team safe. They lived up the hill from the port, in a three-story home with a green door that was sometimes confused with some other house because sailors came knocking late at night looking for women who were not in the house. In the face of repeated insistence by the sailors that they were sure that that was the house they were looking for, Hamid's mother would reply that she was the only woman in the house, and that her only child was a boy. With that, the sailors would look down, uttering some form on indecipherable apology, and walk toward the labyrinthine alleys of the Medina, the oldest part of town, asking for the Green House, as the local brothel was known. Hamid would always feel awkward when such men came knocking, each knock reminding him of the day when he and Lamin found themselves with another group of sailors, not in Tangier, but in the nearby town of Asilah, just a couple of dozen of miles down the Atlantic coast, hanging out with men much older than them, and partaking of a missile-size joint that made the rounds in a cafe by the beach after the two teenagers had emerged from a similar house. The madam was surprised to see the young, beardless Lamin with Hamid and ordered her youngest lady to take care of him, and I imagined the two undressed in the dark, musty room of a dilapidated house, with no heating or hot water, and Lamin summoning scenes from the most erotic movie he had ever seen, *Lady Chatterley's Lover*, trying to be the hulky farmer, or, failing that, the Julio Iglesias he had always admired, and she assuring him that he was the best man she had ever met, and he finding himself suddenly getting dressed and walking out to meet his more seasoned friend, and the two finding their way to the cafe with sailors too hardened to take it easy on him. The two friends developed a soft spot for sailors ever since because they paid for the drinks, besides the free joint, and then let them get out and run wild on the sands of the beach, collapsing with laughter until Lamin thought he was choking. They pulled themselves together and took the coach home, laughing all the way until they returned safe to their families. My father would later tell me that this experience in Asilah left him with a fanatical loyalty to all sorts of outcasts and a conviction that rule-following citizens were types to be avoided at all costs.

"But," my father continued with a smile, "that verdict didn't apply to me, of course."

The trip to Asilah took place two years before Hamid and Lamin took the coach to Fez. It was in Fez, though, that love would be felt for the first time, when the student was away from home, meeting another student from his hometown, now hanging out with bigger groups of homesick Tangerians pursuing degrees in various fields and suffering from the lack of Spanish TV channels in their new landlocked dwelling, resigning to listening on short-wave radios to the games people in Tangier watched in their cafes, thanks to their long antennas placed on the highest roof a cafe owner could find. It was during a group encounter that he quickly saw the petite bright science major, peering out in his direction beyond the hair that covered the left side of her face, smiling coyly, as if she had already seen beyond that moment, beyond the years to graduation, and beyond all the years he'd spend in America, until he would come back to his senses, after a lifetime of loss, to be sure. How could Lamin have known any of this when he stood there, laughing with the group and aching for the moment when he could talk to her alone, looking for signs, any gestures, of hope, and she, with the exquisite skill of her body and deep intelligence she tried hard to dissimulate from her friends, managed to say yes. And so they met, walked, and talked; and she let him run and get lost in other adventures, exploring the various passions he had experienced listening to Julio Iglesias songs, trying to be the romantic he had always imagined himself to be, and the women, with Andalusian and Berber traits, devastatingly luscious, kept pulling at his heart, now strengthened by the dry climate of the city, inflaming his desires, running between this one and that one, chasing fantasies that existed in the songs that he and Cabeza had listened to a thousand times in the Jbel of Tangier until, after three years, he collapsed in the hands of his first love, the petite Tangerian with the same soft hair, the same kindness, and the same fierce loyalty she had shown him before his escapades. And now came the biggest risk of all.

"You decide whether I go or stay," he said.

He had obtained a full scholarship to study in New York.

And she, still looking into his eyes, replied, "Go!"

That was the most fateful decision of his life. He thought of ships sailing to Troy and Christopher Columbus crossing the Atlantic, hitherto the ocean of death and darkness, heading toward the unknown, not knowing whether he would come back alive, in chains, or be the same to the woman who was now setting him free, risking the life they had imagined together, entrusting it to a continent from which no traveler ever returns whole, and she granted the permission with the same coy smile she had used to greet him for the first time.

"What were you thinking?" Rubio asked rhetorically five years later when Lamin knew he sacrificed his love on the altar of American temptation. "Like father, like son. Maybe worse. There is no soul there."

Rubio had known Lamin since the day the high schooler started patronizing the cafe. At first, the blond peasant, whose asymmetrical face, with a nose twisting in one direction, the mouth curved in another, eyes of different sizes, and brown, uneven teeth punctuated by a gap here and there, gave the kid a break from his notorious hustling, but soon the van driver who made a living helping smugglers get in and out of the Spanish enclave of Ceuta asked the student for a four hundred-dirham loan, promising to return it with interest in less than two weeks. Other patrons warned Lamin not to trust the shady character, swearing that they had loaned him money and never saw it back again, that sooner or later he would get his due, what with the growing ease with which people killed each other these days. But Lamin was too proud to be swayed by such warnings, so he gave Rubio everything he had and hoped for the better. He had grown believing that a man is his word and if men failed to live up to that principle and forfeited their honor for the sake of fleeting advantages, it was their loss, not his, for doesn't God favor those who return to him with pure hearts? Nothing else matters, his father had told him during the one and only time they talked about religion. And Lamin's courage paid off: Four weeks later, at exactly seven o'clock in the evening, when the cafe was full and the waiter stood guard over his customers arranged like passengers on a bus, Rubio entered the cafe with a large plastic bag, stood in front of all the customers, blocking the television screen with his head, pulled out four one hundred-dirham bills, walked toward Lamin who was sitting against the wall in the middle, almost the same spot I would find him in more than thirty years later, gave him the money and the plastic bag, and said: "Here's your money, with interest."

Lamin checked the bag and found a thick, Spanish-style towel, Heno de Pravia soap, Aqua Velva aftershave, and a bar of Toblerone chocolate.

"Thank you," he said.

"I am the one who thanks you!" Rubio replied. "You may be young, but you are a real man. Better than these empty heads," he said pointing around the cafe. "They know nothing about Rubio. Don't listen to them. They have no balls."

A couple of men leapt to their feet to give it back to him, but Rubio walked out to the terrace, lit a Marlboro cigarette and ordered a mint tea. Lamin, meanwhile, was somewhat stunned as he sat there recalling what his father had once told him: "People spend their lives, waste their brains, and go to all sorts of trouble trying to deceive their hearts. They want to be tough in order to handle our cruel world. They harden their souls and, in the end, if they are lucky, gain the filth of this world and, before they know it, turn into dust. Don't follow them, son."

Why this thought came to him right at that moment was hard to fathom, but it clearly showed the influence of his father, who had his own Spanish tales to tell, not of contraband goods that flooded our streets and markets, but of love and romance on the Mediterranean.

There was Rubio now, ten years later, long after Lamin had left for America, sharing his opinion again, this time foretelling trouble with women. But Lamin was too young, vibrant, and boldly headed for some kind of success to heed such doomsday predictions. He laughed it off, although he knew that he had lost his first love in the five years he had already spent in America, engrossed in the dazzling life of New York and forgetting the trust that had powered his wings. Rubio's words were doubly uncomfortable because he also reminded him of his father Bashir who had passed away three years earlier, three days after Lamin came home to say his final goodbye. Would Lamin follow in his father's footsteps? It was too early to tell, for Lamin was only twenty-eight when Rubio reminded him of his father's fate, not yet forty-four, the age when Bashir married, for the first time, his mother Zohra in 1959. He had a good sixteen years to be free before he tied his fate to that of a woman. For now, he had ample time to dream without worry and explore the world America had opened up for him.

"I grew up," Lamin would later tell me, "knowing that my father was a man who straddled the cultures, prejudices, customs, languages, and even beliefs of Tangier effortlessly, as if he had been born with a cosmopolitan gene, physically incapable of adhering to one way of life. He grew up in the Medina, the old, wall-enclosed and fortified city, whose gates opened to the four directions, including the port. He was one of thirteen children, born to a fisherman and a woman from the Rif, and was left alone to do as he pleased. A Jewish neighbor took him under her wings and taught him to read and write in Spanish, giving him the opportunity to find employment virtually everywhere in the international city until, after World War II ended, he was hired as a barman in the *Hercules*, a ferry that connected Tangier to Malaga in Spain. By that time, he had indulged in every vice the city had to offer, including smoking cigars and drinking cognac. He even claimed to have been the first Muslim in all of Morocco to have drunk Tequila. 'It was from the hands of a true Mexican,' he always added. Whether he met the Mexican in Spain, Tangier or on the ferry he never explained. When I discovered Mexico and almost never returned, I thought of my father and his experience."

I remembered my own grandfather but could not see him mingling in Bashir's world. He was a *faqih*, a man devoted to religion, the heir to a long line of *faqihs* who migrated from the countryside of Anjra. His life was all prayer, reading the good books, and doing a little business.

"What are you thinking about?" Lamin asked, noticing that I was a bit distracted.

"Oh, nothing. Just my grandfather, and how different he seems to be from your father."

Lamin smiled.

"Oh, yes. A world apart. Just like I am with your own dad."

"Yet my dad says you are more alike than not."

"That's the magic. Even your grandfather was closer to my father than it might appear. In Tangier, lifestyles are personal matters. But being Tangerian, growing up in this city and breathing its air, walking its streets and being whipped by its winds, let alone living in the same neighborhood, as your father and I did, makes us brothers of sorts. Children of *Hercules* and Tingis. Progeny of Zeus. This is why people fall in love with Tangier. They feel that they are in a different world, half real, half supernatural. You feel alive, you go to work sensing that you are suspended between heaven and earth. It's like we are constantly blowing out of a genie's bottle. This is why I have returned. My soul had shrunk to the size of a raisin over there."

I kept thinking of Bashir, wishing I had known him personally and heard him recount his own stories. He would have told me about how *Hercules* gave him access to the best bars and women of Andalucia and ended up spending more time there than in his home port because, as he used to complain, "There is no love is this austere land."

Within a couple of years, a Spanish woman with long dark hair, bronze skin, who walked like a horse about to take off, fell in love with him and embarked on the ferry, crossing the Straits of Gibraltar back and forth until people on this side of the Mediterranean started worrying about Bashir's safety, knowing all too well that this kind of Spanish love either withers in old age, reducing the lovers to diminishing figures walking around the main plaza of the pueblo, or results in madness, murder, or suicide. His stays in Tangier, where he was left alone, gave him respite from the furies of Spanish passion, but as soon as he returned to the ferry, the flames were relit and the drama of a woman eyeing him during the whole trip resumed. After nine years of this ordeal, he knew he was going nowhere on that ferry, connecting the continents and chaining him to the Straits. He needed a strong incentive to quit his job. That's when he spotted a twenty-year-old nurse at the Spanish hospital in town. He could tell that he was in front of a local beauty, forged in Tangier's unique climate, with a slim, tan body, curly hair, a face that hinted at otherworldliness, and lips without the slightest trace of malice. He stalked her all the way to her house in the Medina and, the following day, wore his best English suit and presented himself at the door with flowers and chocolate asking to see her father. When he was ushered to the upper floor of the house, he found a sick old man with a bright white beard lying on a bed. He was a legend in town, having married many women, ran a strange operation providing protection to European fugitives, and preferred to spend time with black fortune tellers. Bashir knelt, grabbed his hand, and kissed it. The old man knew who he was, so introductions were not needed. Bashir went right to the point.

"I am here to ask for the hand of your daughter Zohra."

The old man looked intently at him and replied: "Has she accepted?"

"I haven't asked her yet. I just saw her yesterday."

The old man called his wife and asked her to go check with Zohra. Five minutes later, the mother returned with a big smile affirming Zohra's consent. Six months later, Bashir, who had found a job as a barman at the Caid Bar in the Hotel Minzah, married her in a ceremony that left most of the city stunned. Anybody who had known Bashir was certain he was going to end up a lonely bachelor. They had no idea that the forty-four-year-old man would get one of the most coveted young women in the city, one who spoke three languages and whose regular handwriting looked like refined calligraphy. She had already declined the offers of four men, including the son of the Mendoub, the Sultan's representative in Tangier, and a Spanish businessman who was willing to convert to Islam for the honor.

The following year the couple's only son was born, delivered to the world by an English doctor right in the middle of the city.

"I was born in an independent nation, with strong traces of the colonial past. The whiff of cosmopolitanism permeated the air of the city, our school had French teachers, many bars were still owned by Spaniards, and my father presided over a shady but classy group of patrons at the Minzah."

"Just the hotel alone!" I interrupted.

"Yes. Yet another example of how love shapes history. Do you know the story?"

"Not really. I know that the Minzah was built by an Englishman, right?"

"Something like that. A Greek man, actually, who claimed to be American. He fell in love with a married woman with two children in London, so they eloped to Tangier and set up a place here and one in the mountain, the Perdicaris house that has been restored recently."

"And your father ends up working in the place associated with this man? What a story!"

"Oh, there is more to it. Way more. Maybe another time."

"I had the best childhood you could imagine," Lamin told me the day after the soccer game, when we met at eleven in the morning in the same spot I had found him the day before. He pointed to the narrow alley down the hill from the cafe and said: "Once you get into Brazil Street, you are in the district of Msallah. That was my universe, all the way to Cinema Maghreb, Campo de Sherif and the Spanish Hospital. Only the hospital is left now; the other landmarks of my childhood have been built up. Like someone poured concrete in my brain to block memories. It was at the Cinema Maghreb that I discovered Charlie Chaplin, Clint Eastwood and Bruce Lee, and it was in the Campo de Sherif that I played my first official soccer game. We learned to play on sand, not grass, let alone the artificial grass on the fenced soccer turfs that have proliferated throughout the city. For us, the grass was in the big stadium of Marshan, Campo de Souani, and Campo de Pradar. That was it."

I tried to imagine his childhood, like I often did my father's, in a bright city with open fields and very few cars. I had to get his childhood right because I had the suspicion that it would explain everything, including his return, and the courage to leave a whole life behind. My father had told me about his education at the elementary school Tariq ibn Ziyad, the Ibn Batouta middle school, and the Ibn Al Khatib high school. Like all children, he suffered the normal bruises of childhood without difficulty, but it was asthma that almost knocked him down.

"*Sder*, chest, was the word for it," explained Lamin. "It felt like drowning, or, perhaps, how I imagine waterboarding to feel. Every winter I braced myself for months of no sleep, trying the kindness of my mother, who took care of me night after night after night, until dawn, then made me breakfast and sent me to school. For me, life was all about breathing freely, a pleasure that I never had, although things are much better now. My nostrils are almost blocked; it's a miracle that I manage to breathe."

"Did you get any medications for that?"

"Pills and injections, prescribed by Dr. Serrano, until he passed away."

I asked how the illness affected him.

"I knew it was a gift from the heavens. It allowed me to see and feel people. It softened my heart and made me vulnerable to the coldness of others. I knew a fellow sufferer whose father got him married in high school before he lost the capacity to breathe altogether. When I heard that, I made a secret deal with God, asking for time to breathe easily, without suffocation, and let me go at fifty. I am now way past that, but I remember the year I hit that age. What a miracle. Yet how easily we forget how things might have been."

Lamin stopped. The rays of the late morning sun covered his upper body. But he still managed to look outside, squinting a little without contorting his face. The boy had lived closer to death than his friends ever realized, and yet he refused to use an inhaler because a pharmacist told him if he ever took it he'd be addicted for life and would become helplessly dependent on it. He was told of people who had traveled to Rabat and Casablanca and realized they had no inhaler and had to race all the way back to Tangier. So he toughed it out, coughing, wheezing and teasing his nostrils with feathers and thin paper rolls to sneeze and relieve his chest from its tightness, until the day his parents, out of desperation, took him to a *faqih* in the shanty town of Bukhash-khash, near the state house. That experience, too, would remain engraved on his mind.

"I sat in front of an old man with a long, white beard and a gray *jellaba* inside a dark tin hut after my parents and I were forced to bend so low, almost crawl, to enter its small door. My healer was sitting against the wall at the right end of the hut, darkened from view. In front of him was a tray with two bowls, one with some kind of water and the other with natural ink, the *smaq*, with which children used to write the Quran on their wooden tablets. My parents pushed me in his direction and sat near the door. I walked till I got close. He ordered me to sit.

'Where's the pain?' he asked.

'Here,' I pointed to my chest.

"He murmured a few words, poured some water in the bowl with ink and started mixing. Then he dipped a reed pen into the ink, took a piece of paper, and started writing. He put the paper down near him to dry and gave me the bowl."

'Drink!' he ordered.

'The ink?'

'Yes. The words of Allah. Drink!'

"I closed my eyes and drank."

'Give me your head.'

"I sat on my knees and stretched my head across the tray. He held my face and showered it with three rapid spittles. He then mumbled a few things and asked me to sit back again. He asked my parents to come closer. He picked up the piece of paper with the fresh ink, folded it into a small, square shape, and gave it to my mother.

'This is a *hjab* to protect your child against evil eyes. Put it in a leather pouch, sew it tight, and let it hang down his neck. The pain in his chest will go away with the seasons and become like a lost-long friend. It will reappear only when you think it has gone for good. Nothing ever goes away and nothing stays forever. This illness is not one. It is how our Lord has opened up the heart of your son. He can see now because his sight is almost keen. Almost because he is still alive. Your son will grow and flourish under your gentle care, but if he leaves the land of Muslims, he will be at the mercy of forces beyond my power.'

"He paused a bit, gave me a long look, and said: 'This is your home, my son. You can leave now with the grace of Allah.'"

"My father put a few coins in a bowl near the door and we squeezed out of the hut into the sunlight. A week later, the talisman was hanging around my neck and stayed there till I went to Fez to study. It was there that my body blossomed, my blood quickened, my heart expanded, and my imagination took off. I was in the best of shapes when I sat down with Si Yussef at the end of 1979. When I lost my *hjab* in a hammam, it was a sign that it was no longer needed, that the blessing, the *baraka* had ran its course. Even then, before I pierced the *dark blue heart of mystery in the westward horizon* and took off to the land beyond the Hafa precipice, I knew the rest of the *faqih's* words would reveal themselves in time."

We talked for a good two hours without realizing it, interrupted only by the fifty-year-old Mjido, the morning waiter who seemed to be a peasant who was still maladjusted to city life twenty years after he had migrated from his village. His clothes and demeanor suggested that he slept in one of the ugly construction trucks that crisscross the city and country carrying sand and aggravating drivers of regular sedans and SUVs behind them. These Ford trucks were like prehistoric creatures that had proven immune to the laws of evolution; but like mint tea and Coca-Cola, they were part of the country's national heritage. One never knew the men who drove them, where they came from, and how they ended up driving such monstrous vehicles. I was reminded of all the professions that don't make it in any student's occupation wish list, like crane operator, customs official, soldier, hotel housekeeper, and so many others that give sustenance to a high percentage of the human race but who walk in and out of our lives invisibly, like ghosts who work on our planet and live in another.

Or it may be us, the writers with degrees, professionals with bourgeois aspirations, reputations to make and protect, who are the superfluous ones, living only as an excess, a surplus, stumbling on our appetites and ambitions, wrestling with the demons of competition, fighting stress, and endlessly plotting moves and stratagems, until we end up being drained, exhausted, bitter, angry and good for nothing.

I told Lamin that I had already researched his background and that I had enough information to write something about him, but that I would need no more than a week to fill the gaps and get the story right. He agreed to meet every day at eleven in the morning because that was his optimal time to think. He also wanted to know what exactly my plan was.

"I don't know yet, Si Lamin. It's not your biography, that's for sure. Our talks could inspire a sort of novel, but it may very well be off the charts, not the kind people expect. When I think about your writings and the events in your life, I think we could draw a picture of the clash of civilizations, in the deepest sense of the word, at the micro level. Or maybe we could do more than that, I don't know. I could end up with the usual themes of love, war and peace. Or I could find the answer to my own questions, which direction to take, how to think about the world, how to live, and where."

"And how to die, too?" he asked playfully but seriously.

"I wasn't there yet," I answered with a smile.

"My feeling is only when you get there do you acquire the mind and courage to write. I am not talking about commercial writing, titillating thrillers and science fiction stuff. I am talking about transformative writing, the kind that takes you away from yourself and delivers you to the unknown. It's a bit like the *faqih* in Bukhash-khash. The words that you write go right to your heart—the rest are drafts."

I looked down at the floor, trying not to reply fast, making sure he knew that I was contemplating what he said, not just doing conversation.

"Think of the Quran," he kept going, to break the silence and relieve me of my awkwardness. "It is a book that everyone reads or recites, but the Quran says that the real book is a tablet preserved in heaven and many believe that it existed as such since the beginning of time. Which means, what we have here is only the published version."

"I didn't know. . ."

"I know," he interrupted me. "You are going to say that you didn't know I was religious. The point I was trying to make is that writing is like the vulgarization of feelings, vision, something that exists in a heavenly tablet, a soul that floats in a different realm. When you write from the heart, without fear and without ulterior motives, such as seeking fame and riches, you get close to that realm, and the realm opens itself to you, feeding you with its aura and giving you the right language and voice. In the end, the best writing is not for humans, but for demons."

"Demons?"

"Spirits, maybe. Think of them as your main audience."

"I'll try."

"And one more thing: Keep it short. Give your readers room to imagine, add and change."

"Ok," I agreed reluctantly.

He got up, patted me on the shoulder, handed Mohamed a bill and walked out. It was around two in the afternoon and I was hungry. I followed him and started walking toward Fez Street, facing the massive apartment building that was built recently and where Lamin now lived amid dozens of tenants who used their apartments not as main residences but only pieds-à-terre, as the moneyed class call their second or third homes. Not Lamin, though. He was home here, with a window looking down on Msallah with the old houses and alleys of his youth, and another one looking in the opposite direction, toward the expanding development along the Tangier bay and toward the hills southeast, the glittering Hilton, and the new train station that launched the fastest train in Africa to Rabat and Casablanca. Whether in Cafe Smara or in his new residence, Lamin seemed determined to remain below the radar, to vanish into nondescript crowds, to watch and not be watched and, as I would later realize, to think without being bothered with the concerns of the cultured classes.

I had a quick lunch at one of the popular restaurants down the street, ordering chicken with olives and preserved lemon, along with a bottle of Oulmès, the ubiquitous sparkling water. Twenty minutes later, I strolled down the street to Cafe La Colombe, walked upstairs, opened my notebook and jotted down an outline for my book. When I was served my small glass of light coffee, I looked out at Hotel Rembrandt facing me and, beyond it, to the Straits of Gibraltar, closed my eyes, and could almost see the young promising student flying over the Straits for an overnight layover in Madrid before he takes off for good to New York.

NEW WORLD

Lamin should have had a glimpse of his future while he sat in a Madrid hotel beholding a large group of fun-loving Brazilians reflecting a kaleidoscope of skin colors and an ebullience that was neither African, Mediterranean, or Portuguese. They were a species all their own, as if they were descendants of a different race, born without Old World constraints and allowed to grow up naturally in the paradisiacal habitat that Iberian adventurers conquered almost half a millennium before Lamin set sail for New York. He knew that the United States and Brazil were vastly different nations and was seized by a pang of relief knowing he was going to the most prosperous country of the two, a place that, if nothing else, would impress his friends back in Tangier. At that time, New York was known to Moroccans as a movie set only, where giant buildings harbored free, geekily-dressed, gum-chewing people. He was not prepared for the sight of cops with their heavy gear, coffee to go in a paper cup, and an urban diversity that hid the horrors of racial segregation in the hinterlands. He didn't know it at the time, but he would later discover that New York was a city-state-on-the-Hudson, built on Dutch foundations, not the

Little House on the Prairie that was the iconic image of American bliss. He arrived in a modern city, but he saw with the eyes of early French settlers, like St. John de Crèvecoeur. He was free at last in the rugged world of abundance.

"Crèvecoeur arrived in America around the age you and I did. He was not yet in his mid-twenties, did all sorts of things, was naturalized, like I was, married, like I did, then got caught up in the politics of the American and French Revolutions, suffered, lost, tried to connect his two countries, like I have. Is it a coincidence that, in the end, he died in his native France?"

I was taken aback by this literary excursion and seized it as an entry into our exploration of his—and my—new world.

"It's amazing that we can find parallels in the eighteenth and nineteenth centuries. Your mention of Crèvecoeur, as he came to be known, reminded me of the few Frenchmen who were attracted by America's promise of freedom, wrote about it with flair, then packed up and returned to France. You get the impression that for them America was a nice idea, not a place to live in."

"Touché! That's definitely true of the Marquis de Lafayette, Alexis de Tocqueville and any of the recent and contemporary philosophers who have dazzled naïve American professors and their graduate students with fancy-sounding ideas and returned to their good French lives and wines to watch the effects of their intellectual prowess from afar."

"What would America be without the French? They have a way of injecting traces of high culture in desolate places, like swampy New Orleans, for example. Yet Americans have a love-hate relationship with them, and nothing but filial love for Britain, despite the wars that separated them."

"The French generate this self-defeating response in others. Not sure how they manage it. We also have a love-hate relationship with them. It's got to be that way. Spain could have been a better model and ally, but Spaniards are not Cartesian colonialists. Too much passion to sustain a functioning empire. Still, they are our first economic partner in the world. Let's talk about this later because I want to keep talking about America now, this new world that frightens and entices."

The amazing gifts of life! Who would have thought that two Moroccans would be sitting in a cafe in Tangier and having this kind of conversation? Crèvecoeur had always been required reading for me and now, it turns out, for Lamin, as well. Looking at Lamin as a latter-day Crèvecoeur was not hard to imagine. After all, Lamin, too, wrote about how great America was, compared to the Old World and its vacuous pretensions. But, in the end, they left. Well, Lamin may not have been quite there yet, with his wife and son still living in the States; still, he had definitely taken the first step.

"I was wondering," I started by breaking the silence, "what might be the equivalent of writing letters from an American farmer today. Tweeting about America? A podcast with Uncle Sam? Crèvecoeur's kind of literature is simply not possible today."

"I wasn't thinking that at all," Lamin replied before I was even done speaking. "I was thinking about the French retirees who move to Morocco in huge numbers for an affordable lifestyle. That says a lot about Morocco. The French are quite picky; they don't immigrate, not like the Spaniards, Italians, or most Europeans. But I was also thinking about what La Kenza, my friend's mother, told me before I left for America—that Americans are the children of Gog and Magog, they have no roots, just a congregation of *mlaqteen*, rootless nobodies, trying to make it in a new land. I never forgot that moment: A woman who had never left the country was able to describe what it took me decades to glimpse. In a way, La Kenza's description explains why America could only be the republic it is. You need a way to bring people with no common heritage or memory together. The Pilgrims on the Mayflower devised a compact before they even landed on Plymouth Rock. People without shared culture submit to what they call the majesty of the law. Have you ever wondered about why Americans, the freest of the people, are, in fact, the most servile?"

"Now that you ask, yes, I did. They are terrified of the law and public opinion. I noticed a deep anxiety on the part of my educated friends and their family to look respectable and above reproach."

"They do. Jefferson may have tried to erect a wall between religion and government to avoid hypocrisy, but hypocrisy is the name of the game. It's as if an invisible *agent de police* is monitoring everyone's acts. Don't take me wrong: What begins as an American trait ends up being a global phenomenon. Just like the craze for fitness, it will come here, through the agency of the old copycat classes, our well-educated, global citizens."

"Talking about public opinion reminds me of the tyranny of the majority. In a way, democracies of the American sort reduce people to their lowest common human denominator in order to have a functioning society. You end up with a nation of law-abiding citizens and millions of inmates, all living under the shadow of a vengeful law."

"Lots of violence everywhere. That's what it is. One reason I am back here."

We remained silent for a minute before Lamin started again:

"You know, your talk of majorities reminded me of Tocqueville who, much like Crèvecoeur, had much to admire in America. But he was appalled by the specter of majority rule, which exerts an implacable tyranny on citizens and, basically, severely punishes difference."

"Yes. American democracy, in the end, produces a frightening mediocrity that the Frenchman couldn't abide. He wished for a democracy cleansed from its American pitfalls. What's amazing to me is that Tocqueville was able to get America in a few years, while to me America is always two steps ahead. It is hard to capture, although I totally agree with the author."

He paused for an instant, then asked: "Did you know that Tocqueville also predicted that democracy can't be applied to Muslim societies governed by the Quran?"

"He did?"

"Yes, but he also predicted that Islam would have no chance in the modern age of democracy and enlightened values. He had no idea, did he?"

I smiled.

He added: "That's a subject for another time."

Our conversations in Cafe Smara were reminders that we were in the here-and-now, they were reality checks on my wandering imagination, going all the way back to 1983, when the twenty-two-year-old man landed at JFK airport in New York, mesmerized by the sights, sounds, and a humidity that made him feel soaked and steamy before he'd find himself shivering in a cold building, his body trying to adjust to temperature swings, taking everything in stride, as he thought "I am in New York now; it doesn't get better than this," and that sooner or later he would be absorbed into the rhythms of this concrete maze and emerge, as he had done back home, in the streets of Tangier and the hidden corners of the Fez campus, on his feet and ready to go. He went through the first month feeling that he was spinning at top speed in a Ferris wheel, the people, sounds, and colors blending into a continuous blur, and Lamin, in his small YMCA room on the twelfth floor, listening all night to police and ambulance sirens, wondering whether he had made the fatal error of sacrificing his secure professional prospects in his country to expose himself to hybrid people who seemed to be made up of a mix of steel and rubber.

Suddenly, he got worried.

"I could still go back," I thought, "but then I got seized by buyer's remorse, the reluctant immigrant's dilemma. I had said too many goodbyes, impressed too many people with my new address, created too many expectations in those who looked forward to seeing me become a writer, thinker, or whatnot. I learned then that immigration is a one-way street; it's like going to war. You can't just walk back. Not sure if you grew up with the story of Tarik ibn Ziyad, the Moroccan general who led a small army across the Pillars of Hercules, burned the ships after he landed on the opposite shore, and put his men in front of two options—victory over the enemy or death. There is no going back. The Spanish conquistador Cortés did something similar in Mexico."

"I never thought of immigration in these terms."

"Tough."

Lamin looked up and seemed a bit amused.

"For the first seven years or so, whenever I came home for the summer, my old soccer coach Nehla would ask me what I was doing in America. I would reply: 'Studying.' Summer after summer that was my answer to his same question. Then, one day, he got exacerbated and yelled: 'How long? Even if you were learning the Zabur, you'd be done by now.' The idea of spending many years in New York as a poor graduate student seemed like a disappointment, an insult to his expectations. They wanted to see me wearing Ray-Ban sunglasses, green pants, and giving big tips to everyone. That was their idea of Americans. It's still somewhat true today, don't you think?"

"I'd say, yes, although I feel that America's glamor has faded somewhat. I know people who fly out of Malaga to shop in New York and come back. It's like America has turned into a discount empire for brand-conscious shoppers. The movies they can watch on Netflix at home."

Lamin laughed at my comment. I pulled out my iPhone and looked at the time. It was past noon but not one-thirty yet, the average time for lunch in Tangier. The period between noon and lunch is usually fuzzy, like a lost space, where nothing of consequence is supposed to happen. The cafe was bright. Mohamed was sitting by the door, lazily checking his phone. There was yet another nature show on TV but no one was watching.

"How about lunch?" Lamin suddenly asked.

"Lunch?"

"Yes, let me take you to lunch at the Casa d'Italia. Do you know the place?"

"I have heard of it, but I have never been."

Let me show you then."

He got up, walked to Mohamed and paid for our teas. I got up, too, and followed him into the street. We turned right onto Holland Street and started walking toward Mexico Street. When we reached the intersection of Holland and Mexico, he pointed to a row of clothes shops, a little down Mexico Street, and said: "It's hard to believe, but when I was a small kid, we used to come to that spot to find out which soccer game would be broadcast live on television either on Sunday or, occasionally, Wednesday. The place was Bar Chavetas. Long gone. Like it never existed."

He thought for a second: "At least they kept the name of the street—Mexico. When I was kid, I played with friends in streets named Columbia, Peru, Uruguay, all the way up to Mexico. We are lucky city officials kept the names after they found Arab heroes to rename many others."

We turned left on Mexico Street and started walking toward the new mall that once had been Cinema Lux, the place where Lamin first saw *The Godfather* and *The Passenger*, a movie that no one knows or remembers, even though it featured Jack Nicholson, but whose impact on the young man's imagination was even deeper than that of the Godfather or *The Good, the Bad and the Ugly*, even though he had spent his entire life whistling the tunes of these last two movies. *The Passenger* inspired him to imagine his death, where and how, and that is why, I now began to suspect, he returned to Tangier, coming back to die in his own terms, not perish in New Jersey. He had buried a friend in Connecticut and didn't want to go through the same fate.

We kept walking till we reached the Spanish school on the Iberia Plaza, the roundabout that leads to the main directions of the city, and headed toward the Italian compound that housed a clinic, a dilapidated royal residence where all sorts of events are staged, and the restaurant Casa d'Italia. We chose a table at the end of the terrace, protected from the January cold with a thick plastic curtain and a small heater. We ordered salads and fish and the unavoidable sparkling water Oulmès. We felt the sun without the cold and resumed the conversation that we had stopped at Cafe Smara.

There he was in New York, learning the ways of the subway, taking the A train to 125th Street to attend City College, wondering whether he was the last of a breed of students to benefit from this Harvard of the Poor. He found himself in literature courses he never had imagined, exploring the intellectual ideas of the nineteenth century, how thinkers like Darwin, Marx, and Freud tried to solve the problems of the present and design a better future by understanding the past or overcoming its horrors, and he riding the subway back to 34th Street, walking a block to his residence at Sloane House, unable to calm his head, bubbling with ideas, and so he leaves his small room and walks back into the street, to a revival house to watch all the three parts of *The Godfather*, in sequence, one after the other, until he could watch no more. He thought the movies would shelter him from the passions of the flesh, with Laura, the dark-skinned woman with long, jet black hair who had presented herself as half Moroccan, awaiting him at every turn, inflaming in him desires that were surely, surely, unknown in his hometown, and he succumbing with relish, feeling, knowing that he had finally become Julio Iglesias' alter ego, living the content of his songs, enjoying the poetry of the female body, until he thought he was running out of words.

"I couldn't stop," he said, with a slight sense of embarrassment. "My manhood was challenged in a thousand ways. I kept thinking of the days when I hid in the bathroom of Cinema Mabrouk to watch *Lady Chatterley's Lover* and the kind lady in Asilah, when love was forbidden outside of marriage, even though our classical poems never stop talking about love."

He paused to gauge my reaction.

"I know what you are thinking. That the object of love in these old Arab poems, whether Middle Eastern or Andalusian, is a young man, not a woman. That such poetry, just like suicide bombing, is an outlet for the sexually repressed. That women were hidden behind thick velvety curtains, hushed away in harems, shielded from public view, and only allowed to roam inside courtyards."

He paused again and waited for some response. I thought quickly and answered:

"I wasn't thinking of this at all, but I suspect that these men's love poems about women are mere literary tropes, since women, as you say, were hidden away. The Muslim world after the Abbasids was no Ancient Greece with its varied pleasures."

"Oh, no. There'd be the occasional brave woman, but, for the most part, the lands where Islam ruled were one giant convent, surrounded by wily merchants and false worshippers. The parade of women walking up and down Fifth Avenue in Manhattan would have driven these men crazy. They still do, don't they?"

I smiled.

"You are thinking about my life as a young man in New York, the first years," he started, as if to interrupt my own narrative and inject his own words into my story. "To say that there were the best years of my life would be an exaggeration. Those days belong to Fez. It was there that I was awakened to love, all sorts of love, but it was in New York that I consumed my pleasures, over, over, and over again. The most powerful stimulants descended on me like a storm, entrapping me in their intoxicating power, and pushing me deeper and deeper into a full body experience, the kind of which could never be surpassed in paradisiacal bliss. Never. It makes you wonder about the optimal age to be in paradise. Eighteen? Twenty-three? Can't be older than that. Or younger. Because pleasure in paradise will be consumed in perpetuity, including the best cognac you ever tasted."

"Cognac?"

"That's what a man once told me," Lamin explained with a smile. "He was not a wine guy. Cognac was his thing, even though he never had a single sip. I guess because he smoked cigars."

"I see."

"I don't know which came first. Literature, film, theater, wine or love. Too much sensation. I could hardly breathe. Day after day after day. It is amazing what a young body can withstand. There were times when I wished for a break. Just a day or two to restore my energy. Without much luck."

OK, I need to take over a bit. The story could only be told in broad strokes. Even as he booked seats for major Broadway plays, inviting along fellow students, who dressed up as best they could, wondering about the irony of attending such plays for the first time not with a fellow American but with a Moroccan and he simply glad he had such company because how could a man like him ever love if his passion for literature, film and drama were not, at the very least, understood? And yet, at every turn, he found himself with women he could never have imagined, like the Brazilian hair model from Portugal who insisted that he liberate her from the strictures of her Catholic faith so that she might live her sensuality fully and without guilt. And what was a man to do in such circumstances? He thought of her as a fellow tourist in the city and made some time for them to be together, talking about god-knows-what, and he just accepting how things where, not trying hard to make sense of it all. Then, over a drink in the Village, the brief relationship changed instantly, when she explained to him what lupus was. She left with her golden shiny skin, not to work in the fashion industry in Lisbon, but to write postcards that kept arriving month after month, year after year, until one day he received a letter written by her boyfriend announcing that the Brazilian model had passed away. The letter was delivered while he was with a Venezuelan medical student who told Lamin that her father was born in Morocco and was later assassinated in mysterious circumstances, leaving behind a young wife, two children, and a business that was managed by his brother.

"I believed her," said Lamin. "She had the looks to prove it. And the intelligence."

How long they were together I can't remember now, but the Venezuelan became the marker of a period when Lamin couldn't stop thinking about Hans Castorp, the young man Thomas Mann gave us in *The Magic Mountain*, whose love for family is rewarded by a diagnosis of tuberculosis, the ailment that had afflicted his aunt in Tangier and against which he had been inoculated, and how Hans is now condemned to spend many years in a sanatorium, high in the Swiss mountains, healing from his disease only to be released into the deadly prospects of war. Ever so slightly, the bright lights of Manhattan were turning into the flames of passion, and Lamin kept trying to talk to his Venezuelan partner only to be acknowledged emotionally without, however, getting any literary reciprocity. And so, they went, from theater to cinema, wondering what might become of their ambitions in the city that never sleeps.

"My life was killing me, literally. It doesn't make much sense when I say it like this, but there was just too much pleasure for any one human being to handle. It is impossible to explain, really, because the pleasures were and were not of this world. Or, perhaps, I realized that pleasures of the flesh, drink and imagination were all conduits to spiritual elevation."

"How so?" I hastened to ask.

"Well, think of it. The moment you are in the arms of a young, dark-haired Venezuelan woman with honey-toned skin, the sum total of all your previous fantasies, you are no longer of this world. You are somewhat in paradise, experiencing a moment of *houri* bliss, enjoying the promised pleasure that compensates for our fallen state. Then the after-sin moment happens, the fall again, and you are hurtled back to the travails of everyday life, the worries, the exams, the big questions, the small ones, whatever. Forgetfulness is not really allowed; it robs the masters of the universe of their power to remind us of our fragility. Ecstasy can only be a fleeting experience because paradise is not a real place, only a dream, a mere glimpse of our most cherished hopes. That's it. I am not talking about the Garden of Eden; I am thinking of *jenna*, the bucolic garden with *houris* and flowing, pure wine that gives you a buzz but doesn't intoxicate. Kind of like drinking a good Bourgogne."

And so it went for Lamin, right there in Manhattan, Brooklyn, New York, rising and falling, flowing and ebbing, watching endless movies on their first public release day, guided by the unassuming verdicts of Vincent Canby, the *New York Times* film critic that few people remember now, not the more fashionable Andrew Sarris of the *Village Voice*. He met filmmakers at receptions in Lincoln Center, listened to the Gewandhaus Orchestra from Leipzig under Kurt Masur perform Beethoven's Symphony No.9 choral, attended a quartet at the recommendation of his physician, watched Charles Aznavour perform at Carnegie Hall and Bob Dylan at Madison Square Garden before the singer of his childhood, the one and only Julio Iglesias came to town. For that, he got two tickets and invited a French woman he had met at a party, a translator of books, author of others, a psychoanalyst in the best French tradition and a spiritual seeker in the non-Western one who was less interested in Julio than in deciphering Lamin's mind and soul, warning him, after months of frustrated attempts at reaching him, that he would end up dead in America, his body lying lifeless by the Atlantic shore with dollar bills floating above him like hungry seagulls. She wanted to save him then, take him back to the Old World, but he was already in the intermediate zone, between heaven and earth, flesh and soul, one foot in New York the other in Tangier. And it was in that mode that he would be pulled out of the elevator by a black leather-and-boot-wearing punk with a Mohawk into her room, undressing for him, and revealing a softness and tenderness that her attire and style had camouflaged so well, walking like a Nazi soldier in the streets of New York, keeping unwanted gazes away from her, while she, Lamin now knew, could see the world undisturbed, choosing who to befriend. Sometimes, all a fragile-tough woman like that needs is one hour or two to be safely normal before she retreats back into her uniform and into the hostile world that besieges her at every turn.

Then Lamin's professor, Andrew Getzel, a veteran of World War II, introduced him to William Faulkner and Gabriel García Márquez and his life took yet another momentous turn. The dreamy language of the South flared up from their writings, paralyzing him on the spot, making him feel that he was back in Tangier, back in Bukhash-khash, that writing literature is not a mere aesthetic but a vital form of recording a people's history. He was mesmerized by the fate of the Buendia family in *One Hundred Years of Solitude*.

"Not only that," Lamin clarified. "The opening sentence of that book is pure gold. Just think of it. Here is a guy facing the firing squad and what does he think of? The 'distant afternoon when his father took him to discover ice'! Absolutely amazing. One could pay the book price just for that sentence. I have never forgotten it. It has given me strength in tough times. Something like that happens in the opening line of *Love in the Time of Cholera*: Dr. Juvenal Urbino associating the 'scent of bitter almonds' with the 'fate of unrequited love.' If I ever needed an illustration of the glories of literature, I can't think of a better example."

Lamin had a soft spot for the liberal revolutionary Colonel Aureliano Buendía, but he would be haunted forever by Faulkner's enigmatic character Joe Christmas, seeing in him part of himself in its new decadent phase, although he couldn't put his finger on exactly what it was because, after all, there were quite a few differences between the two young men. He had always identified with Joseph Conrad's Lord Jim and wondered whether his fate would end up like his, but that character was a bit different in his Englishness and fondness for remote exotic islands. He shared some trait with Childe Roland who goes to the dark tower in Robert Browning's poem as well as the mischievous characters in *The Canterbury Tales*, but it was Christmas who haunted him to such an extent that he vowed that if he ever wrote a story it would have to be in Faulkner's style.

"I kept sinking deeper and deeper into the underworld of secular pleasures. I just couldn't stop. Strange encounters multiplied. I was exhausted but insatiable, making up for generations of Moroccans who didn't have my opportunity, you know, the people you see around here, clever, creative, and kind but unable to live their humanity fully, not knowing where to find it."

"Well said, Si Lamin," I commented. "People my age are literally torn between their potential and what's possible. I am always impressed by their ability to use the latest electronic devices, being, in that sense, on Silicon Valley or Shanghai time."

"Living in the shallows, with a difference. This is what saves us, in the end. That difference."

As he spoke, he waved to the elegant waiter Farid, indicating he wanted to pay the bill. I looked at my phone; it was around three-thirty in the afternoon, Lamin's nap time. "Nothing," he once told me, "compares to the pleasure of a good nap. The absolute worse hours of the day are between lunch and dusk. They are good for nothing. I'd rather sleep them out than and be awake at three o'clock in the morning. I don't understand this circadian rhythm business."

He exchanged a few memories with Farid and left. We walked in silence all the way down to his residence on Fez Street, wished him a good rest, kept walking down the street and turned left on Musa ibn Nussair. I turned right at the end of the street, crossed Le Boulevard, and sat on the terrace of Cafe Comedia, the place that served alcohol when Lamin was a boy and now proudly serves pizza for the new ascetic modern set. The January afternoon sun was adequately cool but not cold; the sidewalks were less crowded at this non-hour; and the cars drove by so quietly that I almost forgot I was in

Tangier. I ordered a double Nespresso and just sat there, not looking at my phone or talking to anyone. I needed to put my thoughts together.

The tempo kept accelerating for Si Lamin, driving him further and further away from the rhythms of his Moroccan life. Dazzled by lights and comforted by his thick, native emotions, he was able to manage a sort of mental and physical equilibrium, not surrendering to semi-madness and letting his body go completely. American health rituals were not for him. He tried the gym but found its atmosphere oddly dystopian. In fact, the very first time he tried to check out one, he was insulted to his core.

The manager, a clean-cut young man with a physique that was between muscular and chubby, offered to give him a tour, then invited him to his office to sign him up. Lamin promised to come back the following day, but the manager replied by saying, "That's what they all say."

"I am a man of my word," Lamin shot back.

The gym manager had no way of knowing that. The following day, Lamin returned to the gym, only to be told that the manager was in a different facility in Fort Lee, the town across the George Washington Bridge in New Jersey. Having given his word, Lamin had no option but to walk to New Jersey, find the man, and make his payment. The manager was incredulous, perhaps thinking that he had come across a man from a different time, perhaps a different species, using his best sales language to express appreciation for a customer's loyalty that had yet to be proven, and Lamin signing the document and making the necessary payment in cash because it was the only thing he had. As he walked back to Manhattan, he began to wonder whether he could ever make it in New York and

America. It wasn't the first time such a thought had visited his mind, but he was far, way too far, from being able to make sense of his place in this new country, so consumed was he with all the pleasures that offered themselves to him. He embraced it all with extreme gratitude, without the slightest worry in the world, relying on the protection of God and his strong faith in people.

As if the demanding work of graduate education and dissolution of city life were not enough, Lamin decided to take up creative writing, inspired by a short statement Professor Getzel made when introducing him to another faculty member at a graduate student party:

"One never knows. He could be the next Joseph Conrad."

He knew that he could only write stories that reflect his state of mind, not concocted artifacts that feel contrived and polished. He knew that being Moroccan was already a barrier since his Moroccan experience was lived in a different language, but he thought he had found the key in the mystical language of Faulkner, Márquez, and maybe even Conrad himself. He had so much to say—that much was clear.

"At times, I felt that my chest would burst," he said. "I was containing too much."

He had never thought of writing creatively and didn't even know how one started, but he didn't have to wait too long to find out. After a long night at a local bar, heavily patronized by cops, where he had earned some dubious respect for once trying to break up a fight, he came back to his room, summoned every ounce of courage in his soul, braced himself for a confrontation with time and the world, realizing all too well that whatever he wrote, even if it never got published, or even seen by another set of eyes, would expose him in more than one way to the fickle morality of the world. He had never needed so much courage to start anything, not even when he made the fateful decision to come to America, or to surrender to the temptations of the city. He had been until then a private man, carefully shielding his innermost self from scrutiny, not trusting ever in the opinions of the mob—and wasn't it all mob, all the time?—but he remained undeterred, taking his black pen and jotting two or three sentences on the yellow paper pad on the second floor of Sloane House. It was around ten thirty in the evening.

"It did feel like a confession," Si Lamin explained the following day. "The vast eternity of time stretched in front of me, giving me the strange sensation that I am putting myself on the record indefinitely. Writing academic papers is child play when compared to writing fiction because stories are self-revealing. No matter how hard you try to hide behind a character, you are often describing part of yourself, or the self you wish you had."

"I guess that's why art is important. I took a course in photography and the main lesson I learned is how to look. Or see, I guess. I have never seen the same way since. It's like a whole new world has opened to me. Permanently."

"That's wonderful. These are the riches of life. It's like seeing through a third eye or feeling through a sixth sense."

"Exactly. I often wonder whether the people who are with me are seeing what I am seeing, even though we are looking at the same thing."

"Who knows what they are looking at? Sometimes, I wonder whether we ever see at all. We look without seeing."

"Absolutely, Si Lamin. This must be so frequent. In fact, how is it possible to ever see clearly while there are so many hurdles blocking our view? I mean, one night's bad sleep and you can't see well. Not to mention sickness, trouble at home, work or school."

"This is why art is a more accurate language. It reminds you of the nuances, the ellipses, the unsaid, and reconnects you with your true self—elusive, changing, unstable."

"Sounds right. Please tell me more about that very first experience."

"It was a journey into the unknown. Gradually, the pages started to fill up, even though I was hard at work on my graduate papers and immersing myself fully into the New York experience. Writing fiction was like an added stimulant, further enhancing my already delirious senses, because now I knew for a fact that one part of me was living in the realm of the imagination, not tethered to the brick-and-mortar world of the city. The pleasures were fused in a knot. I must have appeared a bit off to my friends."

"I saw a few photos of you during that time. Nothing different from your childhood ID pictures, those you took at Eva Studio in Makina D'Boony. Remember those?"

"What? You saw those?"

"You gave a few to my father and he kept them."

"Ah, so that's how memory works. It is dispersed among friends and family. It needs to be reassembled and reconstituted. I wonder what will come of your project. Can't wait to see the portrait that you draw. Will it be part of me? A composite?"

We paused.

"I'll do my best. This is a new experience for me, as you know, but I'll try to honor your spirit and trust. I am not looking for psychobabble thrills. If anything, I am trying to help myself."

"There is no better reason to write, Rafik. To go back

to my first foray into this kind of writing, the moment I held that black pen I entered a brave new world, one from which I have never been able to walk away. You make a deal with the universe, so to speak, not the average Ahmed or Joe. It's real stuff."

I pictured him sitting in midtown Manhattan, sirens blasting around him, while he filled out his pages with stories, all based in Tangier. He'd come back from school or the library, eat in the cafeteria below, then sneak away to the lounge and resume writing, day after day, unless he was interrupted by the pull of new discoveries, more of the same, women curious about his work, Moroccan men who wanted to hang out in Brooklyn, movies to watch, plays to see, museums to visit, and no gym at all, despite the fact—and this was his first business lesson—he had signed a contract and committed for a year. The pace was relentless, merciless, allowing little time to breathe, but he kept going. A psychology student once walked up to him and simply told him she couldn't believe he could do everything and still look happy. He didn't show any surprise and greeted her with respect, but she would not let go, until she got to the bottom of it, and thus an entire evening and night was spent talking about life and happiness, as if he were a case study, until the bright sun the following dispelled all mysteries and his daytime routine was restored.

"Very often I'd choose to eat in my neighborhood Greek diner, preferring their eggs over easy and home fries splattered with ketchup over anything I could find anywhere else. Life was simple then, without Starbucks, without smart phones, without the Internet and without computers. I had no typewriter, either. That was a costly problem for me as I had to hand in typed papers for my classes. What to do? Well, right there, in the YMCA, a petite African-American lady with a shaved head, a brave soul recovering from cancer (a term I couldn't use then and an illness I couldn't imagine), offered her typing services and so I gave her my hand-written papers (carefully and legibly crafted) and got them back with my name on the margins. Inadvertently, Ms. Brown, became the main witness to my intellectual growth, not American education, mind you, oh no, handing me back my typed papers without comment, as if she had sworn an oath of confidentiality to some typing god, or government agency, until one day I gave her my first story, a short novella, and her face lit up. 'Well, now! Are we writing fiction?' she asked with a gentle smile. I told her I was giving it a try and if I remember correctly she offered me a discount since that was not required academic work. A week later, when she gave me back my story, she broke the secret rules of typists and told me that she liked it and, who knows? maybe someday I would make a name for myself. I would never experience the feeling of holding the manuscript of my story as I did that evening. I felt like my handwritten pages were transcribed and published in heaven and handed back to me by an angel, Ms. Brown. Crazy stuff. I ran to my room to read it once, twice, and then ran out to the bar to read some more."

Before long, Andrew Getzel heard about the manuscript and asked to see it. It made the rounds of the department until one day Lamin received a letter from the famous American writer Grace Paley saying how much she liked it and asking if he had done anything with it. Not knowing who this writer was or what she meant, he kept the letter but did nothing, carrying on with his life in the city, looking for new books to read, new films to watch, more courses to take, limiting his typing only to necessary academic papers, since the cost of typing was adding up and he could not afford to type everything that crossed his mind or wrote on his paper pads. When Professor Getzel heard about his conundrum, he offered to sell him his typewriter for fifty dollars and expected him to type his own papers. It was propitious timing, anyway, since Lamin was about to move out from the YMCA to live in Brooklyn and he would have had no way to reconnect with Ms. Brown. He went to say goodbye and they hugged for the first time. And he never stopped wondering whether she made it past her cancer treatment.

I saw a picture of Lamin on the doorsteps of the house where he rented an apartment, sitting next to a Hispanic lady and her son. His hair was rather long and he looked rather skinny. It was in that first-floor apartment that he started using his new typewriter, typing on erasable paper, then photocopying what he wrote to give his pages a more professional look. Writing had the uncanny effect of giving him a tunnel vision that took him right back to his old neighborhood in Msallah, reopening new memories, names, and events, using them as a starting point to give voice to those who rarely spoke to him or to what they might have thought of the world and people around them. He realized that he was more interested in hidden feelings and thoughts, in ambiguous gestures, hints of powerful human conditions carefully veiled to avoid heartaches, tragedy, or just to maintain the peace.

New York would not let go of him, squeezing him closer in an ever-tighter grip, sending him reeling in more emotional pleasures and pains, and he responding in kind, as if seeking a doctorate was not enough, because he read books that had never been assigned, big ones, too, like *Don Quixote* and *The Bothers Karamazov* and Günter Grass's *The Rat*, sociological treatises that he knew he had to know, like *The Protestant Ethic and the Spirit of Capitalism*, the history of the Federal Reserve, as much as he could of *Das Kapital* and other writings by Marx, and so on and on. Any other student would have complained about the amount of coursework that was required, but Lamin was too voracious to worry, he wanted more, needed more, and more. He kept writing fiction on the side, too, not to publish, but to feel, to remember, to stay alive.

Writing was not enough, though. The live human touch was necessary, vital, and unavoidable. The more he lived in the tumultuous world, the more tortured he was by his conscience, the more conflicted by the devastating promise of Eden, the more inspired he grew. One day, in a literature course, he forgot his setting and simply blurted out that he had loved every woman he had ever met. "How could you not," he addressed the class, "when they seem to have been designed to be the real angels, not the fictitious luminous bodies that populate greeting cards stores?" A Chinese classmate responded that his people know of no angels and no afterlife either. Perplexed, Lamin simply shrugged his shoulders and said, "Never mind." Whatever this exchange meant, he probably had no idea that he was about to fall in love with Jennifer Hanson, an Americanist with a good knowledge of French literature from Minnesota who seemed to have been sent to prove him wrong. Just as he thought that his hedonism had no end and that he had been destined to perish of pure physical exhaustion a single man, unattached to one person and loving the multitudes, he spotted his fellow graduate student in her office, a blonde with soft skin that was more Swedish than American, a shy and disarming look, devastating eyes, radiant smile, a dangerously dreamy demeanor, and a body that was not fully disciplined and whipped into shape yet. They had seen each other before on more than one occasion, but now she appeared like a revelation, seated in that spot just for this fateful encounter.

"Hello, Jen," he said casually.

"Hi, Lamin," she replied.

He asked at first if she wanted to join him for a walk in the park nearby, then he invited her to movies, theaters, bars, hunting for first-edition books in farmhouses on Sundays; they read to each other, dreamt of travel, moved in together, despite his discomfort with the arrangement, and when they graduated and found jobs teaching in two different universities in New Jersey, he knew that the relationship was not a fleeting one, yet he didn't know what to do since he never imagined hooking his fate with that of an American, he hesitated to pop the big question, or even to think about it, remembering his king's advice against marrying outside the culture, and he knew that the king never said anything in jest, that his opinion was rooted in centuries of royal wisdom. Traveling to America to study was one thing, but marrying an American was a journey of a different magnitude. His parents would neither approve nor disapprove, playing it safe when it came to matters of the heart, but he knew that not disapproving was not a hearty endorsement and that they were basically letting him bet on his future and never have to blame them for its outcome. He knew that his father hadn't succumbed to outside temptation, even to the irresistible Spaniards, but here he was, in a faraway continent, thinking of spending the rest of his life with a woman whose genealogical descent might as well have been from a different planet. Angel, indeed. Except for her outside beauty, he had no way to gauge the substance below the skin, the fire in the heart, the passion in the brain, the values that define a human being.

"Being with a woman is enough of a crazy adventure," Bashir told his conflicted son when the latter called for advice, "but being with an American woman is something I can't even imagine. Don't take me wrong: American beauty is special, there is a sparkle to it that is different. It's just that they can't get you, son. If you want to live with that, well, go for it."

With that blessing, Lamin and Jen agreed to have a traditional Moroccan wedding, complete with the paperwork required from the health authorities, the police, the Ministry of Justice, Ministry of Foreign Affairs, and the local court. Only when all the documents were issued and signed, and Jen officially renounced her vaguely Lutheran faith, could the judges marry them in the presence of her father who, for a five-hundred-dollar dowry, handed him his daughter.

"I was there for the whole thing," my father told me. "I was at the henna ceremony, the family-only celebration, then the public wedding the following day, the Andalusian music, the car ride to the hotel, the whole thing. No one could believe it. We had given up on Lamin ever settling down. I just couldn't see him encumbered by the travails of matrimony. He just wasn't designed for domestic affairs or practical life. That's wasn't the Lamin we knew."

The married Lamin returned to a different life in America. His semi-dissolute but intensely spiritual life was somehow behind him as he settled down to discover the infinite mysteries of his wife. Bashir had once told him that if a man wanted to know a woman he should take a good look at her mother, but Lamin had examined Jen's mother and grandmother up close and didn't see anything revealing, for they all seemed to be cut from the same cloth, a culture that went back into the remotest corners of Europe, a place that no one remembered or even knew, but which lived in the body, smile, and soft blonde hair of his wife. "The person in front of you," Lamin told me, "is a complete universe. You really don't need more information than what you actually see—that is, if you can see, of course."

Soon after he settled in his matrimonial life, he learned of the death of his uncle Si Mustafa, the family's sole memorizer of the Quran, a life-long bachelor who was more suitable for the Catholic priesthood than being a single man in a Muslim society, where marriage is an unavoidable evil, and unmarried people are forced to believe that they have failed in some fundamental human way and not chalk up their marital status (or lack thereof) to their inability to connect with people, let alone members of the opposite sex. Or to have no interest in sex. Si Mustafa was a saint in the wrong milieu. He taught Lamin Arabic, a big portion of the Quran, and mesmerized him with his recitations at home and after the sunset prayers at the mosque. Si Mustafa's lyrical style and dirge-like recitation never failed to convey the mercy Allah had for his creation; it made Lamin feel like he was floating down a quiet river, gently heading toward the end, watching the landscape around him as he drifted, waving to farmers, children, pregnant women, old men, and cats, and realizing that a greeting is also a goodbye.

"His uncle's influence on him was deep," my father explained. "It wasn't actually his uncle's alone. His mother's, too. There was this otherworldly strain that ran through that side of the family, crazy holiness. Lamin's grandfather was a prominent member of the Tijaniya order. Just like we are part of the Derkawi order, they were Tijanis."

This world, so close to my father, was so removed from mine. I only knew it tangentially, through the stories my father told us, or those told by my grandmother who liked poetry and was the secret behind the educational success of my father.

"You may not believe this, but Si Mustafa was circumcised naturally."

"What do you mean?"

"His mother found him bleeding one morning; when she checked the stained area, he was circumcised. She was frightened, of course, but when she asked the barber to come check to see if everything looked all right, he shook his head and exclaimed in awe: 'Allahu Akbar! Your son is circumcised.' Years later, when a master of the Tijani order visited their house in Marshan, he fixed his gaze on Si Mustafa and told his father: 'He is one of us.'"

"You don't believe this, do you, father? You are a scientist, for God's sake. An engineer. Such things are not possible."

My father let things cool down a bit. That's how he was—he would let time have its own input in a conversation, especially if it was controversial or, as in this case, unintelligible to a someone of my generation and social interests. Sometimes I wondered whether we were members of the same family and country, even though we lived in the same house and we were very close. The gap between his childhood experiences and mine was so vast as to make it feel that he had grown up in the Middle Ages, when such notions as naturally occurring circumcisions were signs of divine favor, not serious health issues that required medical care or phenomena that needed scientific explanation, as if explaining away such a tragic accident in supernatural terms would console the parents and avoid blame all around.

Instead of answering my question, my father outlined the simple life of Si Mustafa, how he was close to his mother and sister, joined as many funeral processions as he could, spent twilight hours reading the Quran with his soft otherworldly cadences in various mosques throughout the city, how one rich man approached him one day in the mosque he had built and offered to pay him for doing what he did every evening, read the Quran, and how when Si Mustafa politely declined, the man told him: "I am sorry, Si Mustafa, but you have no choice in the matter. We have no choice. I spent my entire life making money and feeling guilty about it. I built this mosque to make my peace with Allah. But that still didn't do it."

"Your good works will be taken into account," Si Mustafa assured the rich man. "Allah knows everything."

"Exactly," said the man. "That's what I thought. I could buy my way into Allah's mercy by building this mosque. Make up for the fact that I never sent my mother to Mecca on pilgrimage when she was alive and healthy. Cleanse the sins from my bachelor days, when I drank and smoked."

"Allah is most merciful," Si Mustafa confirmed. "He knows our intentions and what's in our hearts."

"Exactly, exactly. That's why you can't say no to me. I have been watching you for a while now. You come here for your sunset prayers and stay to read the Quran till night prayers. You have no motive to do this. Your love of Allah and our Prophet is pure; you don't want anything in return. I can tell you have no major sins to wipe out."

"No one is without sins."

"I know, I know. But you are what I can't be. That's it. Help me out by accepting my gift. It would be like you were praying for me. I will give you a monthly stipend; you can do with it what you want."

I was once again stymied by this story, not knowing how to make sense of it, as it seemed to describe a species of humans that I had never met. Strange.

"And that's how," my father continued, "Si Mustafa earned a salary for years, until he stopped going to that mosque."

It was the haunting voice of his uncle that led Lamin to take the tape cassettes of Abderrahman Ben Moussa, the emblem of the Moroccan Quranic voice, with him back to America after his marriage and to listen to his tapes as he drove to work in his car. His heart started softening as his penchant for dissolution was gradually dissolving. As if by design, a devout Muslim colleague started engaging him in conversation, and knowing Lamin's interest in time, quoted the Quran's passage declaring that Allah's time is not that of humans, proving that time is, indeed, relative. Lamin had just read Thomas Pynchon's *The Crying of Lot 49* and Stephen Hawkins' *A Brief History of Time* when he heard that and that was enough to lead him back to a thorough reading of the Quran and to the prayers he had abandoned since he passed his baccalauréat exams. He wondered whether it was a question of age that was bringing him back to Islam, whether the follies of youth were now behind him, but his questions didn't stop him from renouncing his New York ways. He settled into a new life of normal domestic routines until the day Jen called him at work to announce that she was pregnant.

"I was in my office when she called; there were no cell phones then, or, at least, I didn't have one. She called minutes before I ran to my class to teach. You could imagine the state I was in. People usually recall the moment of birth, but I have never heard people talk about the feelings that seize you when you hear that your wife is pregnant. Which makes me think: How would you like to know—yes, to know—that you will be born in nine months? Waiting for your own birth. Making sure you eat well, rest, and avoid stress. Of course, we don't have that choice, but we get to have a sense of that with our own children. I taught my class mechanically, anxious to meet my wife in the evening. That was like act two in the marriage process. The same joy at the news and unspoken dread of the future revisited us. I could tell from Jen's face. This was a huge commitment, a further step in an irreversible journey. What we feel at moments like these is hard to describe because we simply don't have the language to do so. Things like joy, fear, anxiety, happiness, sadness and such words are banal one-dimensional idealistic portrayals of complex emotional states that cannot be reduced to one or two simultaneous conditions. Do you know what I am talking about?"

"Yes, I do. This happens so often, not just in these circumstances. In fact, I can't think of any circumstance in which we are not failed or deceived by our language. I mean, what do say when a Starbucks barista asks you 'How are you doing today?' You can't just reply and say, 'Well, I feel horrible, but I am still going to have my tall dark roast because it makes me feel better.' It's clear that language is not meant to communicate, only to connect, barely."

"You got it. It's like we live in two parallel worlds, vainly trying to connect them through the use of language. See, I think we are all hopelessly alone with our feelings and thoughts. But language is what brings the world to us, giving us social identities and moralities that never stop tormenting us. Language is like a virus; it moves from one body to another in a never-ending vicious cycle."

I nodded in agreement.

"Language," Lamin continued, "is about light or darkness, black or white, not light and darkness, black and white at the same time. Yet, this is how we usually feel. What they call shades of gray, I guess."

That was exactly how he felt when Yussef was born almost fifteen years after he landed in New York. He saw his son emerging into the world and, as he cut the umbilical cord that tied him to his mother, was overtaken by a bittersweet emotion. He was happy to have a child but sad to know that he would have to join the miserable throng of the living, the living dead with their criminal expectations and deadly struggles, sad at those who never stop proclaiming that life is a special gift, that it is worth living, especially if you think that it is a bad deal, as attested by our holy book itself, except, except for those who save their souls in prayer and good deeds. After the newborn—still without a name at this point—was wrapped in a tiny blanket, he took him and recited the *shahada* in his ears. A few days later, he went to City Hall and changed his son's birth certificate from No Name to Yussef, in honor of his favorite prophet and the man who inspired him to write a book.

BLOOD OF NATIONS

"Aziz didn't know how Lamin and Jen could live on their salaries," Linda said referring to her husband. "Madison is not a cheap place for two humanities professors. That may be the American Dream—house, fence, car, some professional success, retirement—for Americans, not for Lamin. He quickly realized that he had to get out of that situation, somehow. He couldn't let him rot in that morbid lifestyle. Daycare centers, shopping malls, softball. I mean!"

I had met Linda and her teenage daughter Miriam in a restaurant in Manhattan early in the summer before I packed up my belongings and moved to Tangier. At forty-six, her hair was still jet black, her brown oval face, with large black eyes, made her look vaguely Mediterranean, perhaps with the hint of some nameless conquistador who had left a trace in Oaxaca, the heartland of her Zapotec people. Miriam was already taller than her, having inherited her father's height and self-assurance. Here were two American women, of sorts, trying to make it without the man who brought them together and who was now an ever-present memory, haunting them for life, they knew, but they were determined to keep going, as best they could, as if they had set up a permanent camp in the cemetery where he is buried, in a never-ending celebration of the Day of the Dead. They exuded ease, health and wealth in that restaurant, but they were haunted by the ghosts of tragedy and trapped in a nation that gave generously with one hand and took violently with another. Non-immigrant Americans sympathized with them and offered all kinds of support, but these Americans didn't know they were carriers of a violent streak that can wreak havoc and destroy anything and anyone on its path. They looked like they could be on a TV commercial, insouciantly happy and beautiful, but they were a bit lost, without anchor, waiting for an answer to their predicament. When I invited them to talk, they jumped on the occasion because they were as curious about Lamin's new course as I was. They wanted to know.

"So he just moved back and left his wife and son behind?" Linda asked.

"That's my understanding. I really don't have all the details. I am going to find out."

"Ah, this reminds me of Aziz. Exactly what he told me before he drove to Madison. 'I need to meet this guy.' His life wasn't the same after."

Linda had told me about how her husband, upon reading an interview with Lamin in the summer of 2001, got in his Mercedes and drove to Madison to meet his fellow Tangerian. It's kind of the same with me. When I read *Si Yussef*, the account of the bookkeeper and his love story with Lucía, I knew I had to meet the author, not as my father's childhood friend, or the friend of the family I had known in Morocco, but as a person beyond social titles. He had always been elusive, even to his best friends, leading some to attribute his indecipherable mood to some undiagnosed medical condition like epilepsy. This time I wanted to know the thinker because I came to trust that of all the people I knew he was the most likely to show me the way. He was to me what the *faqih* in Bukhash-khash was to him and his family. I didn't know exactly what it was.

"I wish we could join you," Linda and Miriam said. "Let us know how it goes."

We walked out of the restaurant near Washington Square Park and I accompanied them for a couple of blocks on Fifth Avenue as they walked, arm in arm, toward 23rd Street, then retraced my steps back to the park that Lamin told me saved Manhattan from becoming another Shanghai.

"As an NYU guy, I am not sure if you ever noticed that the grotesque Fifth Avenue ends in Washington Square Park. It kinda bumps into the arch and stops on its tracks. A guy named Robert Moses wanted the avenue to keep going, not necessarily through the arch, but around it. But that would have killed the park and one of the few genuine public spaces left in Manhattan. Then a great writer named Jane Jacobs fought him tooth and nail and won. One of the best New York stories ever."

I found an empty bench and sat down to collect my thoughts. It didn't surprise me that it was to this park that Lamin used to come every Saturday in the mid-1980s to watch his favorite street comedian, an African-American who gathered a huge circle around him, made fun of every ethnicity that came his way, and walked away with a stack of business cards and what possibly could be a whole week's income. For whatever reason, he always remembered the line about Puerto Ricans. "Ladies and gentlemen," the skinny comedian would say with a dead serious face, "if a Puerto Rican looks at you and asks, 'Hey, you gotta a problem?' you most certainly have one." And it was in this park that he stood up for his classmate who drank beer without a bag and was arrested. Lamin went to the police station to get his buddy out and was told he was already let go with a summons to appear in court. He was ready to testify on the innocence of the student but the case was dropped. Almost thirty-five years later, I was now trying to resurrect him or make out his ghostly presence as he moved around the main circle of the park. It was an impossible task, I knew, but, at least, he wasn't dead. He was in Tangier.

"Look, Rafiq," Linda had told me a year or so before our lunch, "I had never seen Aziz that excited before he met Lamin, and that's saying something. Aziz was all energy. He could work for days without interruption, use every system at his disposal, phones, computers, anything, to keep business flowing. I was amazed at how people like him end up in America. My husband was a pure businessman, but his education, his master's in archaeology kept him grounded, saving him from the fate of the sleazy types, the wheeler dealers. He could make a fortune in one year and lose all of it the next. Then he'd make another fortune. There is no better gentleman, despite his *locura*, his madness. He provided for twenty people in Morocco, year after year, and he paid for my younger brother to go to a university in California. He made lots of money in real estate and he spent a lot of money. Anyway, when he met Lamin, it's as if had found a lost friend and brother. Moroccans are like Mexicans, even worse, I think. Their hot blood is a time saver. What it takes Yankees decades to consolidate Moroccans do in a week at most, sometimes in a single day."

I smiled at this observation and tried to gauge its truth

in my own experience. Once again, I was a bit puzzled by such unequivocal statements. In such moments, I feel like I had lost out on a reality that came to a screeching halt with the invention of cell phones and the Internet. My father insisted, perhaps out of parental care, that my experiences were as good as he and Lamin, or the generations before them, had, but Lamin disagreed, assuring me that such consolations were acts of love that hid misleading truths.

"Technology is a medium that extends, accelerates, and amplifies its cultural origins. You are right that in the age of cell phones and the Internet we have all become hyphenated Americans. I mean the entire world is. Because of these media, we are all obsessed with things American: politics, films, diets, fitness, diseases, social justice, and so on. We didn't have this when I was a kid. We only had great Hollywood movies and we had to wait for a long time before they made it to our screens, dubbed into French. Now, I have friends who watch pirated American films before they are shown in American theaters. It's crazy."

This is why he left, I assume. To look for the places that were still untouched by America's peculiar psyche. He could have found them in America itself, in New York, New Jersey, or New Mexico, but he knew he would still feel contained in an iron cage. He knew he was not cut for the violent spirit that courses through the great American republic, and aging was not going to make things easier for him. He had been shocked in ways that were unimaginable in Morocco, and although he knew that life in his native land would not be easy, he would at least be able to deal with familiar pains and frustrations. The dramas of America had become too catastrophic for his constitution. America was not a country for old

Moroccans. He couldn't see himself surviving another 9/11.

"I will never forget that day," Jen told me that same summer when I visited her in her house in Madison. "All those people. The buildings. The waste. I cried for hours."

"How did Lamin handle it? What did he do?"

"The biggest irony of all is that on that day Yussef was wearing a t-shirt with the word *maghrib* in Arabic. It was Lamin who picked him up from daycare and brought him home. He wanted to give Yussef a jacket to hide the Arabic script on the shirt. That's how nervous he was, we were. With names like Lamin and Yussef you couldn't hide. In such occasions, Lamin used to tell me that he understood how it feels to be black in America. You are what you appear to be, not who you really are."

"Ah, well said, Jen."

"People in this town didn't even think about him or us differently, even though Bill, an elderly neighbor, one of those tough guys who have no trouble bucking trends, walked to our house and asked if we were doing OK. Lamin never forgot that kind gesture, especially since we were the only ones in the entire block who didn't hang an American flag. He used to say that people like Bill made him proud of America and of being American. He had his own idea of America. To him, if a man didn't display the values of a gangster, the cast of characters in Sergio Leone's Western movies, you know, Clint Eastwood, Charles Bronson and those types, they were not real Americans, men not to be taken seriously. I used to find his views amusing and funny, but he is dead serious about them. Ask him some day."

"I sure will. So you just went with the flow after 9/11?"

"Well, it was a difficult time for Lamin. He was

especially disturbed by the black-and-white threat of our political and media narratives. Osama bin Laden's Islam was not his. His image of Islam—perhaps the only one, now that I think of it—was his clean-shaven uncle, Si Mustafa, with his angelic voice, not the harsh tones of bearded Saudis, Iraqis, Afghanis and the like. Somebody—usually an ignorant person, in his view—was speaking for him, or trying to make sense of his culture, and he didn't like that at all. This is, after all, a guy who wrestled with the nuances of discourse and identity in graduate school. The agony for him was amplified. It was quite painful to see him in that state. I never saw him so alone as he was during that time. I couldn't help him; no one could."

I tried to imagine a younger Lamin wrestling with these heart-breaking dilemmas, but so much time had passed by the time Jen told me this story, and America had almost reverted back to seeing Muslims as a diverse group that warrants respect. The massacre of Muslims in Christchurch in New Zealand in the winter of 2019 had such a huge impact on the world that the victims of the white supremacist seem to have been martyrs for the cause of exonerating Muslims from any misdeeds or violence committed in the name of their religion. It was, as you might understand, hard for me to imagine the climate of 9/11 in light of present circumstances.

"For Aziz, it was worse. He fell into a depression and didn't get out of bed for days," Linda added when I told her about Jen's story. "He didn't take a shower for a week."

"Wow. A week? These are the hidden stories of 9/11 that no one writes about."

Linda's face lit up with an expression of triumph.

"Exactly. Only I know. He felt alone, lost in the violent

clash of civilizations. Getting to know Lamin in the aftermath was like a miracle."

"Really?"

"Yes. As soon as they met they decided to start a Moroccan-American magazine. And before you knew it, as it often happened with those two guys, the magazine was published in less than three months and a launch party scheduled in Manhattan. It was just amazing."

"The things I missed! Oh, well. I have seen some of the early issues. NYU's library has them."

"For years after that, they were practically inseparable. The only problem is I got to see less and less of my husband. I used to call Jen, and she'd tell me the same thing. They would just simply leave for Manhattan or Brooklyn for two or three days and return home exhausted and energized at the same time. Aziz slept less and less and did more and more. It's a good thing I had my own activities and didn't need his presence as much. I volunteered, read, took my yoga classes, meditated, and met with my own friends."

"Imagine my plight," added Jen. "Our son Yussef was still a baby, but Lamin would be gone for days, leaving me alone to handle all the chores, not to mention grading papers and preparing for my classes. I gave him several ultimatums then, but we always bounced back. He'd explain to me that it was part of his big project."

"The Islam and the West, America project? The books he wrote?"

"It sounded like that, and, sure enough, he did well in that area. But his project, like Kurtz's in *Heart of Darkness*, was not always clear to me. It took me years to finally get it. I don't think Lamin himself knew exactly what it is that drove him, kept him going. It definitely was not just us, his family. At times, I felt like he was trying to connect the continents."

I smiled thinking of Lamin, like a latter-day Hercules trying to connect not the continents of Europe and Africa after separating them with one mighty blow, but the new continent of America with the rest of the Old World—Morocco, Spain, and what lay east of them— and he knowing that these two worlds had never meant to be together and wondering whether Columbus should have been blocked and jailed in the Spanish makeshift garrison town of Santa Fe, not given the royal blessing to cross the dark waters of the Atlantic and open the gates to a new order that has enervated the word ever since. The more I inquired about Lamin's doings after 9/11, the more convinced I was that he had been seeking the safety of his native shores, looking for the people who left, like he did, to see how they fared across the Atlantic, what fate had befallen them, for he knew all too well that the Columbuses of history end up in chains, condemned to dungeons, and cast aside ignominiously so that historians could later try to gather the pieces and make sense of them all.

He had thought that the days of New York hedonism were behind him for good, but he didn't expect to meet Aziz and be reintroduced to green margaritas and conversations that never end. He had never met a Moroccan man who could go in and out of business with so much ease, never give away his emotions in business dealings, and treat the entire business culture as a dark world of vultures, all chasing big money. He knew he had met the quintessential immigrant, the true embodiment of the American Dream, not people like him—Lamin, I mean—who found their way to a middle-class existence with its sanctimonious morality, its cheap displays of purity and civic consciousness, those who live on the financial edge while talking a big game. He never stopped reading or writing, but he grew increasingly disenchanted with the culture industry, how publishing was being guarded by twenty-somethings without much experience in the world, how newspapers developed house styles and drained every wild idea that came their way of its power in order to speak to a broad faceless audience of middle class types drinking tea or coffee somewhere in America, and he remembered how he had been warned by the work of the German refugees Adorno and Horkheimer, as well as by film historians whose names remained obscure, that America was no place for European-style intellectuals or free thinkers. He had an almost Nietzschean contempt for academic types, the fragile men and women reading newspapers in a cafe or wearing badges at some convention, unable or unwilling to admit the futility of their enterprise, just buying into what was given them, by some famous professor, or movement, or a social expectation. He told himself that he had chosen his professional vocation because of people like Paine, Poe, Fanon, Mann, Faulkner, and Márquez; fellow Moors like Ibn Batouta, Ibn Rushd, Ibn Khaldun, Cervantes—yes, he considered the Spaniard a fellow Moor, too— and Mohamed Choukri. Ideas had to work themselves out in the world before they get stored and buried in libraries, or dispatched to some ghostly existence in the virtual world.

Aziz, in other words, was a Moroccan born to be American.

"America," he told Lamin, "is, first and foremost, a place of—and for—business. Everything else is auxiliary. Just business. There is no point in coming to America if your goal is not to do business."

Lamin, at first, dismissed his friend's views as

exaggerated justifications, but the more time he spent with him, and the more he looked around, the more he realized that making money is what America was about. He didn't see it as a negative thing at all because he thought that for most people money meant freedom, and Lamin didn't need money to be free. It was a matter of degree. Not for him were conversations about cash flow, stocks, return on investment, and endless talk about real estate because living was a zero-sum operation and time spent doing one thing meant no time doing another. That was, to him, the real meaning of investment.

"We are all born with the best capital anybody will ever get: ourselves. What we do with it, how communities and nations use it, is the ultimate question, one that defines us and really tells us what kind of civilization we have. Let's put it this way: A human life is too precious to waste on the pursuit of hucksterism, making money by any means necessary to insure against poverty and destitution. Marx knew this well. You spend time making money at your own expense."

Unsurprisingly, Aziz didn't disagree but neither was he willing to change. In the end, doing business, real estate or academic work took a back seat to finding a way to live the Moroccan life, not like immigrants in enclaves, but as totally liberated and assimilated professionals, moving seamlessly across American cultures and delighting in the stories of lost Moroccans. They spent so much time together that Lamin grew worried that he was missing out on his scholarship and writing, but Aziz dismissed such concerns as petty: "I will give you stock in my company and you will make money when I create a new software to do business. We will be the Google of real estate."

With such a promise, Lamin allowed himself to dream of times when the only thing he would do is read, write, walk, and spend time with Jen and Yussef.

"Eventually," Jen said, "they limited their day-long excursions to Saturdays only, when they made the two-hour trip to Gravesend Neck Road at the end of Brooklyn to go a Russian bath and spend all day with an old Moroccan Jewish sailor, mason and weekend fisherman. I heard so many stories about this man and every time Lamin told them he grew more delighted, as if he had met a long-lost relative. Often, he would come back with a headache, due to excessive time spent in hellish Russian saunas and whatever they consumed at some bar."

"His name was Tony. Tony Castellano. But that was not his real name," Linda explained.

She had gone with Aziz on more than one occasion and had met the man.

"For some reason, he claimed to be Italian, although Aziz and Lamin knew he was Moroccan, because he spoke the *darija* of old, the Jewish-accented type. They figured he must have been from Larache, but they were not sure. His identity didn't matter, though, because all three knew what it was—what he told the Russians was not important at all. They'd spend the day with him as he drank his Heinekens, which he kept in a plastic bag with ice, and snack on radishes and green peppers. They'd join him as a large group of men from several former Soviet republics gathered around him, every Saturday, some for decades, since Tony had been going to that *banya* for at least thirty years. By the end of the afternoon, he'd grow tipsy and start a fight with someone before a bulky Russian from behind the counter would step out and give him a menacing look to calm him down. But Tony, at least the time I was there, would grow more inflamed, cursing and threatening until things quieted down on their own and he left to go back to his apartment in the same neighborhood. Aziz told me that he had once been married to a Syrian Jew and had many children with her, but she turned out to be too mean for him, so they divorced and he remained alone. He told them about a Russian girlfriend who kept him company as needed, but he was careful not to fall into traps, as rumor had it that he had been nabbed soliciting a prostitute by the beach."

"Did Aziz ever bring him home?"

"He tried, going as far as offering Tony the job of building us a sauna in our yard. But Tony refused, saying that there is no point in having a sauna just for yourself. The *banya* is about community; a sauna at home is just about heat. 'Who wants to be in an empty paradise, one without people?' Tony asked. 'It would be cold.' And that was the end of the conversation. They kept going to the end of Brooklyn until the day a Russian called Aziz to tell him that Tony was dead. They never went back."

Publishing the magazine was the central activity that kept Lamin and Aziz connected across state lines, but they cut back on escapades to New York City and focused more on visiting each other or hanging out in local restaurants and bars. As Aziz kept traveling around the world, sending pictures from Asia, Africa and the South Pole, Lamin isolated himself in the basement of his house, immersing himself in reading and writing, emerging periodically to the first floor to play with his son and be with his wife. Being in the presence of his family was almost an adventure because he was learning how to share a house with a category of people who were never part of his household back in Tangier. He had discovered new kinds of love with Jen and Yussef and he knew that love is a massive gift we are born with, but that it only reveals itself when we tie our fate to other people's. Even then, it comes in degrees. Loving a spouse is not like loving your mother or your child. Each is a different kind of love.

"The most difficult love is that of a wife," Lamin explained the following day.

It was a gray day and the cafe seemed eerily quiet for eleven in the morning.

"I have thought a lot about this, but as I do with most things that affect my life, I don't listen to experts. Things like a spouse you have to figure out yourself. No one can help you. Because there is no one like my wife in the world. No one like her has ever existed. Just like there is no one like me. It's like fingerprints. You have two unique individuals, shaped by different geographies and cultures, deciding to live as one in New Jersey. It makes for an exciting tale, but is also a huge risk. The differences are real and unbridgeable, but I had to make the relationship work after we fell in love."

I was reminded of King Hassan and his advice to his subjects. If people only married from within their cultures, they would at least have a tremendous head start and avoid the pitfalls of cultural expectations and feelings lost in translation.

"Of the loves we can experience, marriage love is the most volatile because we know deep down that the relationship is contractual, like a business deal. Your spouse is not your flesh and blood. If we had been in an academic debate, I would have said that my wife is the Other, doubly so in my case. And it's not a friendship, either, because married people have sex and children. Yet, Jen gave me the opportunity to discover a new form of love because I could watch her, day after day, year after year, up close. My mother was the Madonna, immune to the laws of nature, only a saint showering me with love and affection. Jen was a woman—beautiful, sweet, mad, and demanding. It is precisely because this type of love is fragile, even unnatural, that religions and states have devised rituals to encourage the lovers not to give up and jump ship along the way."

Hearing Lamin speak so matter-of-factly about Jen and marriage may sound cold to readers, but his face, tone and eyes glittered with a profound love for his wife. We knew that sacred and precious things in our lives were not really open to this kind of scrutiny, yet Lamin's analysis enhanced the magical effects of love, not diminished them, as if analysis, like the *jinn*, falls into two categories, the good and the bad, one motivated by pure love, the other by bad faith. I had the impression that he was writing a poem about his marriage and wife, not trying to explain his distance from his family, now that he was back in Tangier. Or perhaps we were both skirting around the edge of the real issue, the unavoidable one, the event, or the series of events, that changed Lamin's life once again, and I was looking for the best way to broach it. Our eyes crossed for a second and we paused.

"We talk about the contractual love of marriage, but how about children. Are they like parents?" They are both flesh and blood."

Lamin looked out toward the terrace.

"Interesting question. I don't know whether it has ever been teased apart. Different feelings, maybe? You are somewhat responsible for bringing your child into the world. It's not the same with parents."

"Fair enough. I was hoping you'd write a story about Yussef—not the Tangerian bookkeeper in your novel. I mean your son."

"I did think of doing so. I just haven't found the time to do it. Memories have faded, but you are resurrecting them now. This is the beauty of life. We are keepers of one another's stories. The time has come to tell that one, I guess. It'll go into your book and be preserved that way. Who knows how it will work itself in time?"

How do I start, then? I pictured Lamin watching his pale son at home, wondering if his vegetarian diet was not nourishing him enough, for Lamin was the only one at home who ate meat. I pictured him in the doctor's office having his son checked and blood tested, after which the doctor called them back and told him to head, right away, to the hospital where a team was waiting for Yussef, and then I tried, the best thing I could do, just try to picture Lamin hearing the word leukemia, and then looking down at his five-year-old son who seemed a bit bewildered, and the two driving to the hospital, as if they were merely going to the doctor's office, a trip they had taken many times before, not knowing that they were taking the longest journey of their lives, the few streets that separated the doctor's office from the main children's hospital. Jen getting the phone call and dropping whatever she was doing and driving to meet them. I saw Lamin and Yussef entering the hospital and going to the section they had been assigned and pictured Dr. Alan Kreuger greeting them with his smile, making light of the situation, getting Yussef safely checked and set up in his room, and striking a small conversation with Lamin, asking him what he did, and the doctor replying that he had dreamt of being a Shakespearean actor but then ended up being a physician, and Lamin thinking: Not just any physician, a pediatric oncologist, the toughest job of all, the real battlefield. He thought of Hans Castorp getting out of the sanitorium and heading to the trenches of World War II to join the infantry, the first troops to perish in these wars. I knew all these thoughts, and much more, raced through his head in a matter of seconds, and he was convinced that Dr. Kreuger was the right man for that occasion, without even knowing that he had worked at the prestigious St. Jude's, the hospital named after the patron saint of lost causes, founded by Muzyad Yahkoub, the son of Arab immigrants known as Danny Thomas, to keep his word and express his gratitude to America. A new door to the heavens was slowly opening to him, allowing him to see hidden epics, remember forgotten heroes, rediscover the spirit that bound him to America, and watch in horror as the world outside the New Jersey hospital grew madder and deadlier.

By the time he and Jen sat with Dr. Collins, a colleague of Dr. Kreuger's, the following day and heard that Yussef had acute myeloid leukemia, known as AML, and a fifty-fifty chance of survival, he knew, as he would throughout his life, that his faith in America and all the knowledge he had acquired would be his weapons as he prepared himself to watch his son go through months of grueling treatments and come as close as anyone can get to death. Being in the trenches was no longer a metaphor. The life of his son as well as his own were on the line. He was convinced he could not go on without his son and the hospital staff must have seen that. Within short order, a social worker, who is a member of Yussef's medical team, came checking on him, asking that very American of questions: "How are you feeling?" He immediately thought of André in the film *My Dinner with André*, describing the surreal experience in a hospital where his very old and fragile mother, on the verge of death, was being treated, and a physician emerging from her room beaming with optimism and making it sound that she was doing just great because her arm looked good. It was the social worker's question that reminded Lamin of his alien status, not as a citizen—of that he was zealously proud—in his adopted homeland. That kind of question had a way of cutting him a thousand ways. He didn't understand it and didn't answer. In such moments, it was the safest thing to do.

"I lived with my son in a special room within the children's cancer ward and witnessed the heroic work of doctors and nurses trying to save young, very young lives every day. A whole war to save lives was unfolding right there, in the best hospital of its kind in the state, kids checked in with almost fatal illnesses, some, many, never recovering, and the world outside was in flames because grown-up men, politicians, didn't know any better. But I got to tell you, though. The strangest thing is that during that time, when President Bush was reviled by my colleagues and friends, I developed a sort of hidden kinship with him because I found out that his sister Robin had died of leukemia when she was a child. Every time he appeared on TV, I would look closely at his face, trying to decipher traces of the sorrow that must have consumed him after she passed away, whether his current sober life was an attempt to avoid falling into the abyss of despair. I kept scrutinizing his expressions and language, while the pundits never tired of condemning him and belittling his qualities. I watched CNN in the parents' room in the hallway, not in my son's, for his screen was locked on Disney and other children's channels."

"It must have been somewhat schizophrenic to be in and out of that hospital wing. I have always wondered about these kinds of experiences. I mean, you'd be in a city, next to a police station, courthouse, or a hospital, and life-and-death situations are happening inside, while the world carries on outside as if everything was great. At the end of the day, the people who work in these institutions go back to their homes, while patients, defendants, or the sick may be in very dark places, if still alive."

"That's exactly right. Alan—the doc, Kreuger—shared the draft of an article he was writing for a medical journal, discussing the impact of working with children with catastrophic illnesses on the medical staff. Lots of alcoholism. Suicide, too. The question is why would anyone choose to be in that field? He ended his article by finding solace in the simple fact that he had known the child, his patient. Snatching victory from the teeth of death. Childe Roland to the Darke Tower Came."

I thought of the way he somehow manages to bring literature, history, film and other cultural experiences into his thinking process. He actually tried hard not to do it and stick to an everyman's style, but that was not him. He couldn't escape the knowledge he had acquired over the decades. Dr. Kreuger could see that in him; that's why he shared his writing with him. The doctor also knew that Lamin read everything he could find on AML in children and the British protocol being administered to his son. He had read about the clinical trials and was concerned by the fact there were no children involved. He knew he had no medical training or education, but the fact that his son was being subjected to toxic doses of chemotherapy based on a clinical trial without children was disturbing to him. His son had almost died of sepsis after one round of chemotherapy, so he wondered if the cure was proving to be more lethal than the disease.

"There may have been no children in the clinical trials," Dr. Kreuger explained one late afternoon when he came checking on Yussef, "but we base our treatment on weight, not age."

"I can't tell you how pleased I was by his answer," Lamin explained to me. "It was the very first time the head of the medical team, an esteemed physician like Dr. Kreuger, answered my question without resorting to some medical mumbo jumbo. So I followed up with another question. At that point, he walked to the door, closed it tight, and walked back to me and said: 'I wish I had all the answers. A lot of what we do is hocus pocus.' I instantly extended my hand to him and vowed to exonerate the hospital from any wrongdoing if he gave me his best intelligence. I was tired of seeing the medical staff spend half their time documenting everything. The specter of lawsuits haunts every hospital in America. That alone is a major threat to public health. We want the full attention of health care providers, not scribblers with no imagination."

Lamin spent days in the hospital library, looking up articles on AML and how to prevent infections in patients undergoing treatment. He was able to locate a couple authored by one Raouf Khouri. He printed one, but the other one, with even more relevant information, he couldn't find. He looked up the author who turned out to be a physician at St. Jude's and sent him an email asking for a copy and advice if possible. He got an automated response, the kind that says "I am out of the office. For help, please contact so and so." He resigned himself to dealing with what he had when, the following day, he got an email from Dr. Khouri in Beirut, of all places, expressing sympathy for his son's illness and promising to get back to Lamin as soon as he returned to the States. A few days later, when the Lebanese physician contacted him with questions, Lamin found out that Dr. Kreuger had been the mentor of Dr. Khouri. Still, Dr. Khouri sent the missing article and added an email with a list of actions to prevent infection after the next round of chemo. The doctors at the hospital had promised Lamin that they would have a plan, but when Yussef was about to undergo treatment and the doctors didn't show any plan, Lamin refused to let his son go through the treatment. He was summoned to the doctors' office, where Dr. Collins asked why he was taking such a radical and dangerous measure. He said that he just couldn't let his son go through another life-threatening procedure if nothing was going to be done to prevent infection. Yussef couldn't withstand another sepsis. This was a battle for life. He then produced the instructions he received from Dr. Khouri and asked Dr. Collins if she had a similar plan. At that moment, the conversation changed. Lamin became a partner in the treatment of his son, with the full blessing of Dr. Kreuger.

"See how the world comes together around an illness like this. Our Jewish doctor, Dr. Krueger, is the mentor of an Arab doctor at St. Jude's, a hospital founded by an Arab immigrant. My son was surrounded by nurses and other physicians who were from different backgrounds. There was one, the head of the intensive care unit who told me he believed in God. When I asked what kind of god he had in mind, he replied, very matter-of-factly, 'The God of the Bible. Old Testament.' This was a man who had seen much death and had come to accept the inscrutability of life, its meaning, and that there was no possible alternative to a god that reigns supreme over his creation—yes, it's a male god."

"Where you concerned by that? Where you worried that the last physician between your son's life and death had those beliefs?"

Lamin looked away, as he always did when such questions were asked. I got the impression that he was going back to his comfort zone, when yes-or-no questions were off-limits. He looked at me again.

"Not at all," he replied. "His words gave me an insight into the man he was. I didn't see a dangerous crusader, but a man trying to cope with suffering, tragedy and the limits of medicine. To me, it's never about what people say they believe or don't believe. It's knowing their souls. Humans are a fragile lot."

Yussef survived the worst trials and the most lethal round of chemo, the last super dose, because Lamin was able to identify a soothing and protective substance to shield his son from the worst toxic effects. Dr. Kreuger ordered the product and Yussef sailed through the entire episode almost unscathed. After seven months, Lamin, Jen and Yussef took a picture with Dr. Kreuger and were discharged. Lamin remembered the moment his son was born, in that same hospital, five years before and wondered what future awaited him. He had expected the tumult that is the lot of every human being, but he had not expected it to visit his son so soon and with such ferocity. As the Majritis walked out of the hospital into a nice, sunny September afternoon, Lamin remembered again the sort of Hans Castorp and the various big wars of the twentieth century. Deep in his heart, he knew that Yussef was walking out of the hospital only to find himself—sooner or later— in the trenches, an infantry boy, young man, grown man, and, fingers crossed, old man facing the colossal might of fate, which we think can be managed and even controlled through the use of science or, failing that, reason. Lamin was hoping that his son was walking into a long future, now that he had paid his dues to the toxic effects of modern civilization— and that he had been somewhat vaccinated against the horrors to come.

And yet, Lamin was also walking out of that hospital in a state of extreme gratitude, in awe of the many forgotten men and women who through their creative work and deep humanitarianism, had saved his son. He was grateful to America and its people, the many kind neighbors, teachers, colleagues who had rushed to help and do whatever was necessary to relieve Yussef and his family. He told me about pictures of his son and another child with a different leukemia posted on supermarkets and around the neighborhoods advertising a bone marrow drive to find a match for both of them, and how a couple of his colleagues at the university volunteered to be tested for a match. This was an especially difficult episode for him to recall because the other boy never made it, forcing the highly emotional Jen to attend his funeral service, having to hug his parents and give them her family's condolences. Many years later, Lamin would run into the father of this unfortunate child at a teacher conference in Yussef's high school, in a classroom where Yussef had no idea about his teacher's identity while the teacher knew all-to-well who Yussef was, reminding him each time he saw him of his own son. I learned that catastrophic illnesses, or maybe even regular ones, produce their own shared secrets, things known but unsaid, as if everyone abided, naturally, by the same medical vows of confidentiality. Despite my mostly untroubled life, thanks to my father's diligent care, I realized that illnesses, even minor ones, were gentle reminders of our eventual demise, ghostly murmurs in a gym, ominous winds in an Olympic stadium, and horsemen of an impending apocalypse.

"There were people who considered Christopher Columbus's discovery of America as the second act of creation," Lamin commented on my ruminations, which were only obliquely made visible, "and I considered my son's illness my own second birth, not to mention his, of course."

"How so, Si Lamin?"

"I experienced a whole bunch of feelings, very intensely, as if things were coming to an end. I suspect you know the Morocco saying, 'When a drummer beats faster, it's a sign he is about to stop'? It's like everything in life. The more intensely you feel something, the most likely that experience is about to end."

An image came to mind but I didn't dare share it with Lamin. He wasn't looking at me, but I was sure that he was reading my mind, somehow. He smiled knowingly.

"It's not just lovemaking," he started, "but really everything we do. Like writing the best sentence in a novel or line in a poem. The moment you realize that you have been spared torture. Unrequited love. You fall in love, hopelessly, desperately, hoping that it will be reciprocated. But, in the end, it doesn't matter that much. Or I should say it's a question of degrees. Whether your love is reciprocated or rebuffed, you won't experience that same emotion again, being in love and being in a state of utter suspense awaiting a response, a reaction. The first taste of an exquisite meal. Walking out into a glorious late Spring day after a good night's sleep. Swimming in the warm waters of the Mediterranean without being bitten by jellyfish. Getting a job offer. Winning the lottery. See what I mean?"

"I do. It's like we live for the ephemeral moments of pleasure and spend most of our time, our lives, in waiting mode, or just merely existing. Drudgery is our fate."

Lamin smiled again.

"The only remedy to this drudgery is an active imagination, sustained by deep compassion and nurtured by reading literature, history and philosophy, when it's not dry and pretentious. It's the only way we can make the most of our lives."

I thought for a second and said: "I get it." I added: "What was the major lesson you learned from Yussef's illness?"

"It's all about blood. For seven months, I sat in my son's room, watching him tethered to blood bags, with unknown people's blood flowing into his veins, tiny drop after tiny drop, replenishing the life source that had been drained from his body after each chemo treatment. Hundreds of blood bags, all carefully tested, flowing into him, while he waited for the white blood cells, with their protective agents, the neutrophils, to build up naturally and protect him from the elements, infections. For the first time in my life, I was able to see blood differently, not as a sign of injury or the spooky fluid of massacres, but as a life-giving force, allowing my flesh-and-blood son to survive. I thought of Genesis and its emphasis on blood relations, genealogies, and realized how primitive that concept was, powerful but tribal in the extreme, because people didn't know what they would later know, that blood is a common heritage, like a river flowing through the veins of humans."

He paused to sip from his café-au-lait.

"Blood is mentioned hundreds of times in the Bible but weren't it for free thinkers, creative minds, we would still be in the dark ages, fighting and dying unnecessarily. People died for blood and draining the sick from their blood was what people knew. George Washington, for all we know, may have died of bloodletting. Yet I owe my son's life to a long list of forgotten physicians, crazy enough to think of transfusing blood instead of draining it, adding blood into the body, first from animals into humans, causing damage along the way. We are here because European and American medical tinkerers, people like the French doctor and philosopher, Alexis Carrel, known to me during childhood as the author of *Man the Unknown*, crazy for experimenting with clairvoyance, a man whose eyes were of different colors, who learned how to stitch from the embroiderers of Lyon, moved to America, like so many of us do, and saved a baby in New York by connecting the veins of a desperate father to those of his son. Think of that for a second. It happened because father and son had the same blood type, something that nobody had a clue about until blood types and anticoagulants were discovered to collect and store blood and infuse it in people with syringes."

"I had no idea," I replied in total amazement. "It's true, we see things, like planes, and take them for granted. When you look back at how we got to this point, you find a lot of martyrs, crazy pioneers who were driven by some obsession, many dying along the way, until we end up enjoying the comforts of modern travel. Or the miracles of medicine."

"Martyrs is exactly the word. Those who create to make us live, then perish in flames of passion. Who remembers now the Canadian Communist surgeon Norman Bethune who traveled to Spain to fight on the Republican side against the Franco fascist regime and came up with the idea of storing blood in milk bottles and carrying them to the wounded, instead of bringing the wounded to the hospital? Shipping blood to battlefields now precedes any major war. It's one of the most top-secret operations, a sure sign that war is in the making. Once done with Spain, the Canadian joined the Chinese Communists in fighting the Japanese. And you know how he died? He cut his finger and the infection killed him. That's it. Just like that. And the Spaniard Federico Durán-Jordà who collected only type O blood, mixed it with a few solutions and kept it in refrigerated bottles; this is the guy who inspired Janet Vaughan, a relative of Virginia Woolf, to get Britain ready for World War II. Without these people, where would we be? Where would I be? My son, too, of course."

"It must have been disorienting to be in a hospital watching humanity's blood flow into your son's veins and watch the same human beings wage war against one another."

"To say the least."

With his son saved, Lamin returned to his normal life, diving deeper into his reading and writing, taking weekend trips to Manhattan to watch new movies and, when cold, enjoy the heat of the new *banya* he discovered on Fulton Street. He had emerged a new man from the ordeal of his son, with an even stronger sense of the futility of life. He watched Aziz throw himself into new business ventures and travel around the world. Lamin traveled, too, to give talks and give lectures, but he was not a tourist. He was not the kind of man to go places just because they were on some bucket list. He was rather like his hero Jefferson, a worldly man if there ever was one, but a man who also knew that travel is a fool's errand. He kept listening to the Algerian song *Ya Rayah*, gradually sensing, without yet being fully aware of his inclinations, that a man never truly leaves his country, that no place can take Morocco or Tangier out of him, no matter what.

"With the Internet," Jen told me, "his obsession with Morocco became worse. Worrisome, actually. He'd spend hours watching music videos on YouTube, reading the news, and emailing people in Morocco. Just as he was growing to be more American he was, at the same time, being pulled away by technology. He really lived between worlds."

"Why do you think that is?" I asked. "I kind of understand his urge. New York, America can be stimulating, but no one can break the spell Morocco and Tangier have on us. I actually feel bad for those who are forced to live outside the country. Political exiles and self-exiled cultural snobs."

"He was perfectly assimilated, so you must be right. There is something about Morocco—or so I hear. Anyway, whatever homesickness he must have suffered, he more than compensated for it by hanging out with Aziz. Problem is Aziz was getting a bit erratic. Very impulsive. He was promising to make Lamin rich after he creates some kind of software. He never understood why Lamin would waste his time with a bunch of drained, lifeless academics who bring their lunch boxes to work or eat an apple for lunch at their desks."

I laughed at this picture, so familiar to anyone who had walked the hallways of a university.

"And the water," she added with a smile. "'What's with the water?'" he used to ask indignantly. He was shocked at the sight of people carrying huge bottles of water everywhere they went. It's almost as if Americans suddenly discovered that water hydrates, he used to say. To him, the university was an intellectual wasteland, full of rigid professionals and self-important bureaucrats. He thinks that his university experience in Fez, as dilapidated as the buildings were, was far richer than any American is getting for tens of thousands of dollars. So yes, thank God for Aziz. I would never have been able to take care of that side of Lamin. I'd frustrate him with my pragmatic American ways. He used to say that he'd never met an American who was a true intellectual. Not like the French, who fascinated us in graduate school and cast a spell on the humanities and social sciences for decades."

"I can imagine. But I am not sure he cares that much about the French, either. I would have to find out some day."

"That would be great. In any case, with Aziz he was engaging in a different kind of cultural experience. One that meant something to him."

I remembered the story of Lamin and Aziz in a bar in Boston, both drinking beer and Aziz suddenly announcing that he was on the verge of making a fortune with his new software and that Lamin would finally be able to quit his job and live as he saw fit. No more worries about biweekly expenses and car payments; they would live big, enjoy the American Dream fully, and establish a business back home. Now that they had magazine, they could go further. Lamin dreamt of a place where people could visit, relax, and learn, a compound thick with trees, plants and flowers, benches, a restaurant, classrooms, conference room, theater, a place that would attract tourists tired of five-star hotels, bed and breakfasts, riads, rich, educated people who would meet their semblables in an educational environment, just on the edge of Tangier, with access to the Medina and the new city anytime. In no time, Aziz had a Turkish colleague plan it, a magical place, on paper, while Lamin started assembling professors of Arabic, history and archeology, the most surprising of the disciplines, because almost no one thinks of Tangier as one of the oldest cities on earth. What did Mark Twain call it? The second oldest? Whatever. I remembered the story Lamin told me about his childhood friend, another unsung martyr, Ahmed Sadiki.

"I had known him all my life and we were puzzled when he chose to major in archeology in Belgium, and we thinking, what is that? What will he do with that? Until he came back, many years later, working in the ministry of culture. One summer, I met him in Le Boulevard and we decided to talk at the beachfront bar Las Tres Carabelas. After one Flag Special, I realized how archeology, with its rocks and traces, is a major threat to Islam. Ahmed had written about Lixus, the Carthaginian and Roman site south of the city, near Larache, which still had an amphitheater and the frightening mosaic of Poseidon, god of the oceans. To simplify things and tell a straightforward story, he said that Lixus is the place where Hercules headed to acquit himself of one of his twelve labors, fetching the golden apples from a tree guarded by a serpent, which is why he had to cross the strait separating Spain from Morocco, wrestle the giant Antaeus, trick him and break his back, marry his wife Tingis, and proceed to the place where Atlas holds the sky. It's a myth, our own, but it all made sense. Our city was named after Hercules' trophy. As the hours got later, Ahmed whispered that the story of the serpent in Adam and Eve's story is universal, found in other traditions and mythologies, but to say so in an Islamic society is to court trouble, and so he limited his work to explaining what the Roman sauce of garum consisted of, why Romans came fishing in Tangier, why Roman emperors prize a seashell from Mogador that produced the perfect purple for imperial togas, and how the entire city of Tangier, the old one in the Medina, is sitting on layers of civilizations. And it was Ahmed who fought corrupt city officials when they granted building permits on historical sites, draining his energies and making powerful enemies. He kept losing his prestigious jobs until he landed a professorship and almost vanished. But I kept finding him, as I still do. He has, singlehandedly, pushed me into an unknown world and opened new gates of discovery and knowledge. That's how I discovered Atlantis, Plato's tale about a vanished utopia, so much so that I once wrote a paper about the cultural history of the Straits of Gibraltar. What I owe Ahmed is incalculable."

That's why Ahmed was chosen to be the major instructor in this Tingis compound; he would tell a story that is conveniently forgotten.

With plans this advanced, the two friends boarded a Royal Air Maroc flight and flew to Tangier to find land for their project. Lamin was ready to leave his tenured faculty job at the university. Jen was supportive since she was ready for a change. And both parents wanted Yussef to grow up in Tangier, get some of the Moroccan warmth and learn languages before it was late. Linda, too, was happy to move to Morocco, be near Spain, and live away from the stereotypes that weigh down the best of us. In Morocco, Aziz and Lamin located a perfect piece of land on the road to Asilah and returned to the US to make further plans. As the summer approached, Lamin and Jen planned a vacation in Maine, renting a two-bedroom little house in Saco Beach for four weeks in July. It was a place, like much of New England, that attracted a special breed of vacationer, people like Jen, not Lamin, because the ocean was cold and the sun rarely hot. Then there were the mosquitoes and horse flies that made sun bathing a very tricky and exhausting activity. This Yankee paradise was definitely not Lamin's.

Still, they settled into a nice routine of walking on the beach and going out to eat at Yellowfin's, a restaurant on the edge of Ocean Park, a dry Baptist village sandwiched between the sedate city of Saco and the very wet and wild

Old Orchard Beach. Aziz and Linda, who was pregnant, came up to visit on Yussef's eighth birthday before flying out of Boston to Mexico City. After a great couple of days together, and as plans were further consolidated for the compound in Tangier, the couple left late in the morning. It was an unusually sunny and hot day, so Lamin slathered himself with tanning lotion, despite Jen's repeated objections, sprayed bug repellent on his ankles, and laid down to sleep, hear the waves, smell the ocean and pretend that he was by the Mediterranean facing Spain. Jen stayed in the house to write syllabi for the courses she was teaching in the fall, while Yussef was watching shows on TV. Hot and sweating, Lamin gradually fell asleep and started dreaming of his childhood, friends, beach, hammams, and school until the *faqih* of Bukhash-khash appeared like a gothic character, out of nowhere, so vivid, so alive, looking at him with those stern but caring eyes, just looking, and Lamin wondering what the man was there for, what he wanted to say, why now, but the *faqih* kept looking at him, almost like a grieving mother, until Lamin getting sweatier, twisting and turning in his siesta on the sand, laying there in limbo, in an infernal paradise that is neither home nor away, still trying to figure out why the *faqih* was there, what he wanted to say, why this presence. In his dreams, he heard his cell phone ring, stop, ring again, stop, and then ring again. So much so that he was awakened from his delicious slumber and dug into the plastic bag besides him, took out the phone, and, not able to read the screen because of the strong sunlight, answered. It was Linda. She was almost incoherent.

"Lamin, Lamin. Aziz is dead. Aziz."

"What?

"He was shot dead by an air marshal. They killed

him. They killed my husband. They thought he was a terrorist."

Dazed, still in a sort of sun slumber, he looked around to see if the beachgoers had heard what Linda just told him. But it was all beach bliss.

"Shot? Killed? Terrorist?"

"Aziz had a manic episode. He thought he had left his phone at the gate and forced himself out of the plane to get it. The marshal asked him to stop but he kept going. They just shot him dead. Just like that."

I had forgotten to mention that Aziz had been diagnosed with bipolar at the time he was telling Lamin about his grand plans for wealth, but the two friends joked about this fancy illness and associated it with geniuses and legendary military leaders like Alexander the Great. Aziz had been prescribed lithium and other medications, but they never talked about it. To them, it was just another inconvenient chronic illness, like high cholesterol and high blood pressure.

"Please come down. It's terminal A. They want to talk to you as a person of interest."

Within thirty minutes, as the terrified Jen and Yussef looked on, Lamin got in the car and found his way to the highway.

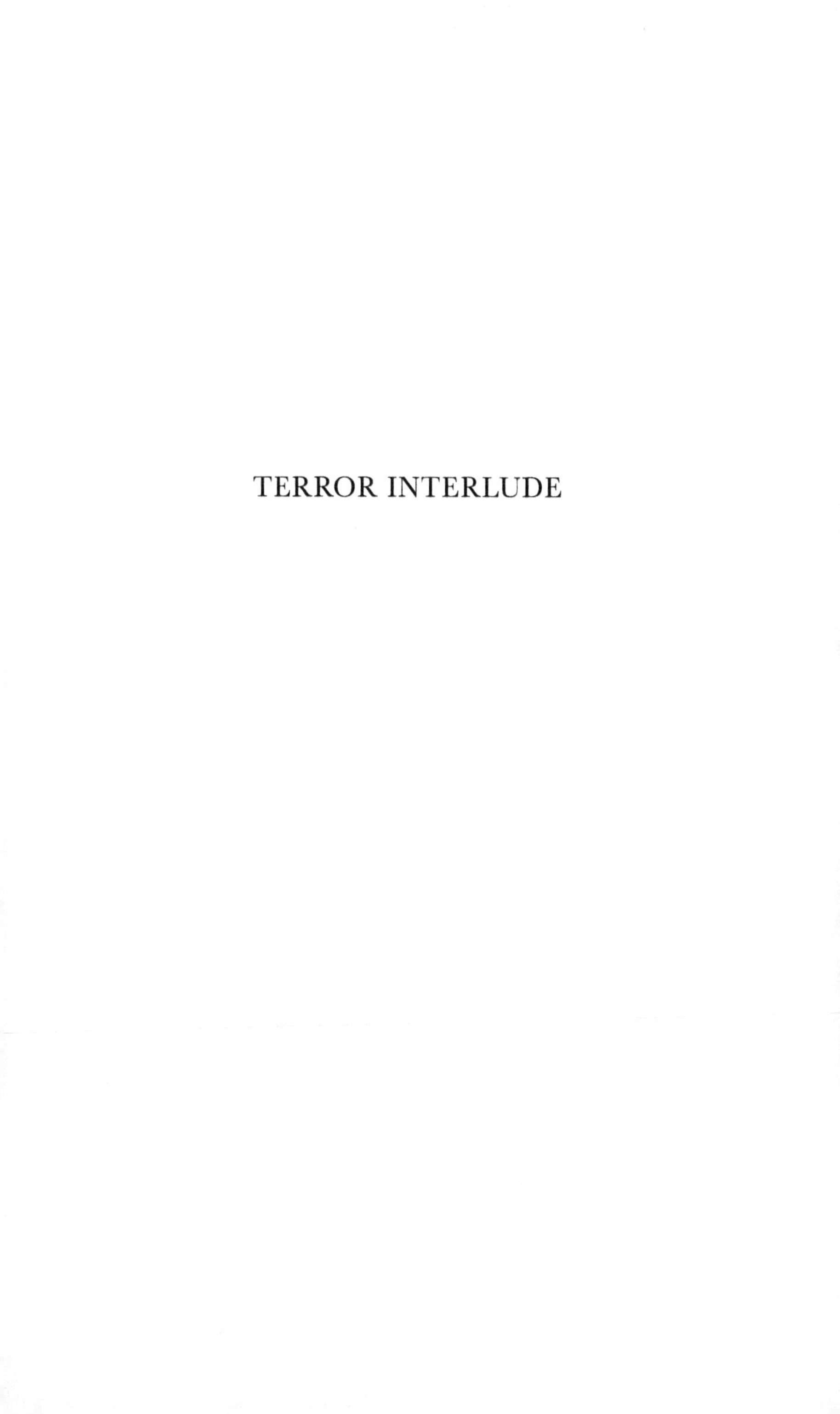

TERROR INTERLUDE

A moment of respite turned out to be an infernal nightmare on the steamiest day of the summer. Lamin was understandably edgy—and how could he not be? Can you imagine being in his place? Driving on the highway where state troopers were on the lookout for the slightest infraction? He imagined being pulled over and trying to explain why he was speeding. "Excuse me, officer, but the Arab-looking man and suspected terrorist who was shot at Logan today is my friend. I am on my way to the airport to see what is going on."

"Cars are moving traps in America," Lamin told me. "They are like confessionals on wheels, driving people right into the hands of the law."

I was lucky I lived in the city, not having to drive or own a car.

Lamin lightened his step. He wove his patterns through the heavy traffic flowing south, thanking the unsuspecting drivers who allowed him to trail their speed without risking being caught. His foot quavered over the accelerator while his mind was shrouded in thick fog. His heart pulsated with anguish—he had no idea what he was driving into. He tried to breathe and relieve the tension invading his body, but he couldn't think his way out of the obvious: He was about to become some kind of material witness. A witness to what? He didn't know. The only thing he knew—had known—was Aziz. He had no idea where what happened. He turned on the AC. To fortify his nerves, he tried listening to 1970s Moroccan group Nass al Ghiwan on his tape player. The songs that were once revolutionary now sounded too self-conscious. Nothing worked. At that very moment, as he was navigating the rush hour traffic on I-95, he was on his own. Sort of like Columbus on his maiden voyage. Or he might have been in some rendition facility. He barely existed as he knew himself.

By the time he reached the end of Maine, he was exhausted from the anguish and clashing thoughts racing through his head. The radio, too, didn't help. It seemed that everything that came out of it talked about Aziz, Morocco, Al Qaeda and terrorism in no particular order. His life was suddenly wrapped into a dark cloud of horrors. He now seriously feared that he might not make it all the way to Boston. His body was getting weaker by the minute. His vision was blurring. He reached for his glasses in his glove compartment while navigating the traffic but couldn't find them. He gave up and kept driving. He needed to do something to remain steady. So, as he crossed the green-painted bridge into New Hampshire and saw the pale evening light reflected on the Piscataqua River below, he decided it was time to shut out the noise. He turned off the radio. He even felt strengthened to know that he was entering a state whose cars proclaimed that it was better to live free or die.

"Someone," Lamin explained, "some politician once wanted that motto changed because it cast the state in a negative light, because such language gave the

Granite State an aura of too much independence or violence, I don't know. It wasn't good for tourism, the politician said, but the people refused to go along. And so Maine's neighbor welcomes people with the fervor of revolutionaries, not the slick hand of business. This is what I liked about America when I first arrived—the license plates of New Hampshire. Not its opportunistic politicians."

As it got darker outside and he drove toward Massachusetts in his quiet car, Lamin felt a bit of light enter his mind. It was his memory, rather. He couldn't think about his future anymore. He was more like a dead man driving—racing into the arms of the FBI, Homeland Security and the global eye. He wondered what he looked like—whether he resembled any of the terrorists and suicide bombers who appeared with striking regularity in newspapers and on TV news programs. That parade of disheveled men with pathetic stares, the kind of people he and Aziz never gave a second look when they walked furtively through our childhood streets or even on Tangier's main boulevard.

"We could tell that they embraced virtue to strike back at people who knew how to live better. They mingled with us to enjoy and denounce—a strange defense mechanism if there ever was one. But such people were few and were more likely to be *gamberros*, tough guys who walked leaning to one side and smoked hash or *kif* when out of the glitter. These were the guys who would go to prison and come out confessing that they had been had by tougher guys than they. Your father could tell you stories about them. They had no time for religion, unless it was the Melhi variety, the fiery imam who mixed denunciations of state-sponsored lotteries and pleaded with his congregation to refrain from smoking hash before the last prayer of the day. It was the most zealotry we got at the time, until Egyptian preachers and Saudi TV networks started beaming their views into our homes. We should have known that it was only a matter of time before someone got killed. The poison of the East never fails to strike. It had happened more than a thousand years before. Morocco's Muslim founding father, Mulay Idriss, had fled the terror of Baghdad to our country and was honored by local Berbers in Volubilis with a throne. But the long arm of terrorism reached him, even in Morocco. Who hasn't suffered the wrath of Iraq, the mother of all violent nations? Even the mighty Americans, the most powerful nation of all time—so they say—couldn't twist the Iraqi arm. And so the poison of terror struck in Casablanca and Madrid. It struck Aziz dead and threw me into that nightmarish ordeal."

He was crossing the Massachusetts line. He tried to put his thoughts together. They would ask him questions about Aziz and his connection to him.

His cell phone rang. It was Linda. She was still shaken.

"Where are you?" she asked.

"In Massachusetts. I am less than an hour away from Logan."

"Good. The people here know you are on your way. I told them that you are like his brother."

"What is going on right now?"

"I don't know. We can't see Aziz. They have to do tests, maybe an autopsy. He will be delivered to us when they are done."

"Do they know what happened?"

"I think they do, but they still want to talk."

"I'll be there soon."

"Don't worry," she added.

How could he not worry? Trouble seemed to trail him

since he had left Tangier almost twenty three years before that fatal day. He had believed that it was cool to be from Morocco, a Muslim nation that is kept away from the bad limelight by its ancient tradition of moderation in all things. Not anymore. In a sort of cosmic joke, of all the states the mastermind of 9/11 and his accomplice chose to start their mission of chaos, they chose Maine, as if this set of believers were sent to remind us that no Muslim is allowed to enjoy tranquility while the lands of the Middle East were burning with hatred. Would people now suspect him and Aziz of plotting the same thing? He wondered whether any one of them resembled the band of terrorists who caused havoc on that dark September day. Mohammed Atta's broody eyes and misshapen mouth certainly didn't look like his or Aziz's. The Egyptian man was too skinny and small, the perfect body for a sexually repressed architect with artistic inclinations. His accomplice looked goofy in a bank's ATM footage. Neither did they look like Zacarias Moussaoui, the twentieth hijacker, the man of Moroccan descent, as the media, for some reason, never ceased to describe the Frenchman. They were definitely older, but then Middle Eastern men have a way of looking the same age, whether they are in their twenties or forties. Perhaps it was our ageless dark skin that made us all look suspect.

"Hadn't some of the nineteen perpetrators been to a strip joint?" Lamin asked not so rhetorically because, quite frankly, 9/11 was not the main event of my life. "It's always the jihad or porno for Muslim men. Those in between have nowhere to go; they must suffer the whims of extremes. Between a rock and a hard place, the East and West, the North and South. Aziz didn't give them license to speak for him. Actually, we tried to speak for ourselves by starting our own magazine. We have a voice, too. We never voted for an imam or a conservative politician; we were socialists through and through. To think that these two losers were blessed by God to avenge us was more than an insult. Yet they won. They turned us into targets for all sorts of homeland defenders, thereby triggering the spark of resistance that leads ever so imperceptibly to defiance and the false glorification of traditions. We didn't fall for that, but they still killed Aziz through American hands, and now they were pushing me to the brink of madness."

Let any scheming Muslim terrorist take Lamin's place for a second—driving down the interstate to face a phalanx of officers, all intent to dig out his innermost thoughts and intentions. Bin Laden would have never made it. The Islamic State didn't even exist then, so no use talking about them now, although their caliphate was reduced to rubble. Bin Laden was good at hiding in compounds in plain sight. In Pakistan. Until they got him. That was later, I know, but, at that time, he was very much alive. The ghoul of the world's consciousness. Had Bin Laden been in Lamin's spot that long summer day, he might have shouted some medieval slogan or committed suicide en route. Not Lamin: He had a friend and a legacy to take care of.

"Who was this Bin Laden anyway?" he asked rhetorically, once again. "Sometimes I thought he was a mere ghostly figure, a man who lived only through some old television footage or a disembodied voice streaming through the Internet. All I know, though, is Aziz would most likely be alive if Atta hadn't come our way years before. Aziz was his victim and testament—forget about the Arabic gibberish found in a parking lot outside Logan airport. His will was my friend's death, thousands of innocent deaths, not some reward in heaven. And it happened all too easily."

Lamin had gotten off I-95 and was now driving on Route 1, a long corridor of shops and businesses that ends in the city of Boston itself. Traffic looked regular—no roadblocks or detours. People seemed unconcerned that a man was shot at Logan. Since it was past five o'clock, they probably were thinking about their families or processing some episode that had transpired at work that day. They were hardy soldiers, those commuters. They did this day in and day out. Then, on summer weekends, they did more of the same, packing their kayaks or bikes to spend a day or two in Maine, the Wild West of New England, the vacationland with rugged nature and oceans to revive dulled senses, lining up in front of the New Hampshire toll booth, a line that stretched as far as the eye could see.

He got off Route 1 and carefully negotiated a treacherous traffic circle and veered right onto the road that leads to Logan and stretches into the American Legion Highway. On his right, he could decipher a grocery store with a big Arabic sign announcing *halal* products. He wondered about the courage of businesses like these. Why not take the sign down and put one in English?

He reached the airport zone. Police cars, ambulances, and fire trucks were flashing their lights. The terminal from which Aziz and Linda were flying to Mexico looked like a military base, with uniformed officers everywhere. Flights landing in and taking off from the terminal had been resumed, except for Gate 17, where the shooting had taken place. He drove slowly around the terminal and asked a trooper if he could park on the curb since he had come to help with the investigation. The state trooper spoke in his walkie talkie and soon a man in a suit appeared. Courteously, he asked Lamin to park in the terminal lot and walk back through a bridge. People were waiting for him at the gate. Once safely parked, he approached the gate and noticed a number of officials milling around or just standing. He couldn't relate what must have been going through his head and racing through his veins. You can imagine. For a long moment, he thought he would never make it to that gate. His legs felt weak and wobbly. Then he heard his name and a scream. It was Linda racing toward him. He ran a few steps toward her. They hugged. She was in tears; he was not. He never cries on death occasions. He was reminded of the images of Iraqi women on television crying over the death of their loved ones, next to a pile of smoldering rubble.

"The passion of Linda made the officials in the airport look like extraterrestrial zombies, lifeless bureaucrats with ice-cold blood in their veins," Lamin told me. "I knew that's why Aziz fell in love with her, after years of pleasure with prostitutes, married women, and blonde Americans. It was like homecoming for him—only a Mexican wasn't quite Moroccan, Arab, or even Spanish. Five hundred years of European conquest have not erased the Indian in her. She was more than Mexican. She represented a spirit that has long left the world. Except in a few places. Something primordial. Honest. A genuine specimen of the cosmic race."

Lamin remembered the day when Aziz told him about his wife. "Wait till you meet her," he told him jubilantly. He didn't say *see*—he said *meet*.

"A subtle but loaded difference because one meets Linda—one does not just see her," Lamin explained. "When Jen and I met her, she told us about growing up in Queens. We learned about her parents' origins in a village in Oaxaca. How they entrusted their honeymoon to a coyote who smuggled them into Arizona, leaving them dehydrated miles away from Tuscon. But they made it and soon crossed the country after a lengthy stop in Albuquerque. The road to New York took much longer than the one they had taken from Oaxaca to Arizona. Her father had once told me that speed in America actually slows you down."

But everywhere the new couple went they could work. The gringo planet—her father's expression again—was made abundant by the Anglo invincible will. Years later, when the government announced amnesty, they walked away from their fugitive lives to become legal resident aliens. Then they applied for citizenship. Thus, America was re-made again. Beautiful, modern, and fashionable Linda assured Lamin and Jen that America will never empty out of Indians. "We are here *hasta el fin del mundo*."

Her belly showed; it made her look nobler somehow. As they held each other's hands, a man, probably in his sixties, with a brown jacket and eyeglasses approached them discreetly to make them understand that he was Lamin's contact, if that is the right expression. He didn't look threatening at all, but he looked intelligent, someone you can't fool. Something about him brought back memories, but there was no way Lamin could make them out in the intensity of that moment. After he and Linda finished consoling each other, he walked to him with a stretched arm. Another man, in his thirties or early forties, appeared next to him.

"Hi. You must be Mr. Majriti—Lamin Majriti," started the first man.

"Yes, I am. You may call me Lamin."

"I am Frank Santucci. This is my colleague John Blanchard. We are both with the Federal Bureau of

Investigations and have been assigned this case. I am sorry about the death of your friend. If you don't mind, we need to talk to you to make sure we understand what's happened today. This may take hours, so we booked rooms for us at the Hilton nearby. I hope you don't mind."

Lamin looked at Linda. She gave him a rather enigmatic look and made him understand that they had already spent hours with her.

"Are you going to be around when I am done?" he asked Linda.

"Actually," Mr. Santucci suggested, "you guys can meet tomorrow or later. It would be best if she left now. She needs to rest."

Such concern sounded menacing. He wondered if he would ever go home again. For a fraction of a second, he was tempted to curse Aziz. What had he done? Why was he so stubborn?

Mr. Santucci walked him to a row of seats by a gate and they sat comfortably away from the law enforcement crews assembled in various parts of the terminal.

"Would you like some water?"

"No, thanks. I don't like the taste."

Mr. Santucci smiled vaguely and asked him basic questions about where he lived, what he did for a living, his family life, immigration status, and other matters that seemed quite ordinary. He also wanted to reassure him that he was not in any kind of trouble and that his sole motive was to find out as much about Aziz as possible. Lamin welcomed his reassurance since he had an ill-defined inkling that telling him as much about Aziz would somehow turn his friend into a martyr, not for a particular religion or nation, but for some kind of sanity.

"Such clouded feelings clashed with my mounting anxiety and dread. Images raced through my head,"

Lamin recalled. "I thought about dead men walking to the executioner's chamber being stopped and released into the sunshine of freedom. Switching from death to life could be quite traumatic, if not deadly. Being on the edge of death with my son only two years before, I learned to live with constant fear, but the fright that seized me now was of a different kind, as if emotions, like cold viruses, were never meant to be exactly the same."

"I understand," I replied, just to say something. "You'd think that once you experienced fear, you'd get used to it and be immune to its effects. But such emotions do not follow the laws of biology."

Lamin thought for a minute.

"I grew up believing that our bodies will tell their own stories on the Day of Judgment, our minds and voices, helpless bystanders in this final audit. Logan airport, at that time, felt like my terminus, my final destination. I wished I had been a saint, a man beyond the slightest reproach, for only then would I have the strength to walk through the narrow gate of innocence. I remembered Jake Uphill, my old historian friend who wrote about the American drug traffickers who made money selling opium to the Chinese in the 1800s before they became art collectors, grand philanthropists, and pillars of their society. Jake had worked for a unit of the State Department that was later converted into the Central Intelligence Agency. 'No one,' he used to tell me, 'can withstand a thorough investigation.'"

Lamin needed to breathe. Merely moving his head and catching a glimpse of the wide terminal with its busy spaces gave him the strength to adjust. And just as he had been transported into an unfamiliar zone only minutes before, he landed back on a plane of equally inexplicable serenity. His mood swung back to compensate for the intolerable stress it had undergone. All of this happened in fractions of seconds. Body and mind may be one, but, at this moment, more than any other in his previous life, they seemed to have lives of their own, wholly separate from his wishes. He understood why people surrender. "We really have no control," he said.

As if prompted by an unconscious part of himself, Lamin asked for some time to settle down.

"Since this may take hours, if not all night, I would very much like to have a Starbucks coffee, or at least good coffee" he said. "Is there anyway we could do this?"

"There is a Starbucks near at the end of the hall," Mr. Blanchard said. "We could have coffee here before dinner at the Hilton."

"Great!" said Mr. Santucci. "Let's get started, then."

They walked out of the death scene as if it were the most natural thing to do, as if their walking away was normal procedure. He thought of Jen and Yussef and asked if I could make a phone call on his cell.

"Please do and take your time."

The phone didn't even ring before Jen replied.

"Oh, my God, are you OK?"

"Yes. Just make sure Yussef doesn't get upset."

"Of course, of course. Where are you?"

"I am at Logan, about to talk to a couple of FBI detectives. This may take all night, but they are lodging me at the Hilton. Don't worry about me. I will call you when I have more information. Please, please," I insisted, "don't let Yussef get upset."

"OK, don't worry. I called my parents. Everybody is worried. This is scary."

"I know, but be strong. Tell your parents not to worry."

"I love you."

"I love you, too."

The terminal was bustling with people, as if the tragedy a few yards away had happened in a distant country, too removed from the concerns of passengers and frequent fliers. A few Muslims were part of the crowd. Women with *hijabs*, pushing strollers behind bearded men, walking unself-consciously, as if they hadn't the slightest concern about being Muslim in America. Lamin looked at Mr. Santucci and Mr. Blanchard to gauge their reaction to the presence of Muslims, but detected nothing at all. A million voices had been reminding him of the perils of being Muslim in America, and yet the most conservative Muslims, men with long unkempt beards and shrouded women, walked proudly, confident in the promise of America, its rule of law and basic fairness. Images of the *hallal* grocery store flickered in his mind. He relaxed a bit.

The atmosphere was decidedly tense at the terminal.

"It's one of those moments when 9/11 reappears, in miniature, to remind us that life cannot, will not, be better after that fateful date. The nightmare must replay itself and the fear of terror, of death, must remain constantly fixed in our minds and hearts. I remembered Jen collapsing on the sofa with our toddler in her arms and Tahar Ben Jelloun's *La Réclusion Solitaire* on the couch. She was a mother then and saw the world through different lenses. People were parents or children, and to see such random death was too much to handle. She just cried and cried."

Lamin was frightened, too. When he picked up Yussef earlier that day from daycare with the t-shirt in Arabic, fear and paranoia blended in his shaken mind. He wondered whether a caring parent might report his toddler as a suspicious character. As they drove home, he kept wishing for an encore of the Oklahoma bombing episode, hoping for the culprits to be native-born, honest-to-God, blue-blooded Americans, not a bunch of Middle Eastern looking men, as had been initially reported. But he knew he was grasping for straws. The government and the media had already checked their prejudice and were careful not to repeat the Oklahoma mistake. Deep in his heart he knew that the perpetrators were either Arab or Muslim, or both, and that he would simply have to endure yet another episode of silent accusations. Terrorism, he knew, plays into the hands of the worst bigots and unsettles the most robust of liberal dispositions. What he could never fully understand is why terrorism does this more than war massacres.

"When I arrived home," Lamin continued, "Jen was simply overwhelmed by the radio accounts of the horror. We were spared graphic images because we didn't have television but we still felt in a war zone, certain that the debris and dust from Manhattan had been blown by the furies of that gray day all the way to Madison. In the midst of terror and sadness, I wondered about the ironies of history, which is nothing, in some ways, more than the passing of time. In the 1970s, lonely immigrants in France sought the elusive affection of prostitutes, as Ben Jelloun's old book on the couch, now a forgotten classic, had made poignantly clear. Now it's the wrath of God and the solace of virtue that are being sought for refuge. Times do change."

"How's the coffee?"

Lamin was awakened from his disjointed reveries by this most practical question.

"Oh, the same. Regular. That's what I order all the time. Tall, regular, no room for cream or sugar. This way, it doesn't matter whether I am in Chicago, Albuquerque, or Boston. It's the same coffee. A strange taste of home, away from home."

Mr. Santucci smiled while Mr. Blanchard's expression remained nondescript.

"Never thought of Starbucks that way. One could say the same about almost everything we do these days, don't you think?"

"Yes. I could travel to the other coast right now"—he looked around him at hurried passengers—"and have a hundred percent home food. The national food and beverage franchises' major contribution to civilization—relieving us of homesickness. In fact, I am surprised no one thought of the slogan, 'With Us, You're Always Home.' I . . ."

He paused, remembering the times Jen had expressed frustration at his uninvited discourses on almost any detail that crossed his mind. He often blamed this habit on the toxic effect of his French education in Moroccan schools and the endless cafe conversations in Spanish-influenced Tangier. The French never stop thinking while the Spaniards never go quiet. As he sat drinking his coffee, and they their water, he worried they may get bored, tired, or even offended by his ways. He had to find some way to break the ice, to bring the two men closer to him, somehow, if he were to be valuable to them. An interrogation would bring back images of Morocco's heroes being tortured or exterminated, those who fought the French and Spanish, before he was born, to liberate our country from the humiliation of occupation. A one-sided interview would also offend his cherished American sensibilities, for his America remained the land of revolutionaries who inspired Moroccans and the whole world to fight for freedom.

As Lamin was preparing for the interview, he had

already formed a cultural profile of the two men. Mr. Blanchard was of French origin, perhaps a Franco-American who descended from the hardy stock of Quebecois who streamed across the border more a century before to work in the textile mills that dot the New England region. Theirs was and still is a community of hard work and virtue. He may speak a smattering of Quebec-accented French, or have an aunt or grandmother who still does. Having classified the man in his mind, he turned to Mr. Santucci and asked if he were of Corsican descent.

Mr. Santucci was startled. He may have expected Lamin to think of him as Italian-American, like everyone else did.

"Actually, I am. My grandfather immigrated from Italy, but he was born in Corsica. I don't know much about him, but this much my dad was able to tell me."

"Did he come through Ellis Island?"

"Yes."

"Did they identify him as Corsican or Italian?"

"Italian."

"Makes sense," Lamin commented, wondering whether his silent commentary on the matter was obvious to his handlers. This would have been a perfect entrée into a discussion about the United States, geography, and the Middle East, but who was he kidding? This was the FBI on official business, and he was a person of interest. After all, they probably thought that Aziz was a terrorist. And if he was Aziz's best friend, what else could they assume? He certainly must have good information.

"Listen, Mr. Majriti—sorry, Lamin—we are mostly interested in Mr. Nejjar's life, prior to his relationship with Ms. Santiago Ruiz, but any new information would also be most welcome. We are not in a court of law, but we are federal agents trying to figure out what happened today. We are not doing this because you are of Arab or Muslim descent, but because Mr. Nejjar was a good friend of yours. You are not a suspect in this case."

"That's right," confirmed Mr. Blanchard. "Consider this a friendly conversation, but one that is forthcoming. We need the truth."

Lamin looked at Mr. Blanchard who definitely looked older than forty at that moment. He imagined he had a wife and one child, and perhaps loved to play golf. As much as he was curious about his French-sounding name, something kept him from talking about it. Not that he was the bad cop of the duo—they were none that he could see. It was perhaps his bland expression, or the lack of a strong Mediterranean element about him, that gave him pause.

"I would be most delighted to help in any way I can."

"Thank you. More coffee?"

"Sure. I was just about to ask if I could. Let me go get some. Do you guys want anything?"

"We are all set, thanks."

After a couple of sips and the taste of burnt coffee on his lips, he looked at Mr. Santucci and confessed that he was not entirely surprised by what happened that day. This startled the men.

"What do you mean?"

"Aziz's death."

"Please, explain."

"Well, I have been having a bad feeling about his future for at least two years. I noticed after my son came out of the hospital. He seemed to be on overdrive. He had a hand in many businesses and wanted to succeed overnight. He certainly knew how to make money. But the success was getting to his head. Even his father—

who, by the way, passed away last year— thought he wanted to grab America by the balls."

The men made no comment. They didn't exhibit a response at all.

"He spent the last few months thinking he was building the next Google."

"He really believed that?"

"Oh, yes."

No response.

"He also thought he could change the way people bought cars. Doing away with the middleman altogether, he would allow car shoppers to assemble their automobile as they do a Dell computer. Then they would save it in a cart and buy it whenever they are ready to click. This software scheme included financing. Just as people shop for mortgages on the Web they would do the same as they shopped for the car of their choice. He was surprised Amazon didn't sell cars."

"Did he talk about Islam?"

"Well, yes. Who doesn't?"

"And what did he say?"

"Not much. That Muslims, with all the noise they were making, can't make crap—his expression, not mine. Not even a needle. He thought Arab Muslims were a nation of ditzy consumers and buffoonish bourgeois types who looked down on the poor. He had nothing but contempt for the rich."

"Those were his views?"

"Absolutely. He thought I was a coward for not disseminating my own through *Atlas*, our magazine."

"And what are *your* views?"

"I pretty much share his. It's amazing how much we agreed on. It made our friendship all the more special."

"What did Mr. Nejjar think of 9/11, Al Qaeda, Iraq?"

"This is a whammy of a question. How do you expect me to answer it?"

"Try. It's part of our investigation."

"Aziz condemned all three. Come to think of it, we disagreed on Iraq. One of the few things we disagreed on—we didn't agree on everything, by all means. I wasn't sure it was all bad for the Iraqis to suffer American intervention. Saddam was a psychopath who had to be stopped, even if he had no weapons of mass destruction. The Sunnis didn't care—in fact, they believe that the Shiites are fair game because they are not Sunni. Something had to be broken for that country to be liberated, for the Shiites and Kurds to breathe."

Suddenly, just as the rhythm seemed to have picked up, the two men fell silent, as if prompted by a hidden message, or were suddenly hit by a disabling fatigue or irresistible boredom. They looked out of place, as if they could jump to their feet anytime and flee the scene, never to reappear again. Investigating humans must take its toll, after all. Lamin didn't know whether he was hallucinating, but he began to prepare for chasing them, in case they took flight. He couldn't take the risk of being abandoned by his FBI handlers. That might make him look more suspicious, as if he had a secret too disturbing to reveal. Or maybe they were all tired. His comment on Shiites and Kurds elicited no response whatsoever.

Mr. Santucci checked his watch and said it was getting late, that they had to start going to the hotel to catch dinner. Lamin was told to leave his car at the airport parking lot and drive with them. It would be easier that way, and they could drive him back to the lot whenever their business was done. Obviously, this unexpected logistical decision sent shivers down Lamin's spine. He seriously wondered whether he was going to vanish into some legal black hole and not be able to call his wife in Saco or his family back in Tangier. As they walked to the terminal departure entrance, where a black sedan was parked safely only a few yards away, he realized, once again, that his life had reached a turning point. Logan was his ground zero for risk. He simply had no idea what might happen next. And though he was seized by a mortal fear—the kind that shatters the mind, not concentrate it—the professor, or editor, or cultural commentator in him wondered, vaguely, subversively, incoherently, whether he was being treated to an emotional roller coaster that many Americans would pay millions of dollars to experience. He knew he shouldn't be visited by such absurd ruminations, but he was haunted, I guess. For his thoughts didn't end there. It was at that precise moment when he took his first steps in the direction of the black FBI sedan outside of Logan that he wondered whether violence is the latest reality show in a country weighed down by the drudgery of unfulfilling work. People, he thought, could do anything for a thrill.

"Don't take me wrong," he said, somewhat reassuringly. "I was frightened, too. When we were kids, we were told that upon our death, the archangel Azrail would visit us soon after the mourners leave the cemetery and give us a quick, tough squeeze, followed by a quiz about the essentials of our Islamic faith. The wrong answers would send us to intolerable punishment. The grave test is like a rehearsal for the ultimate trial, when all the living and the dead would assemble for the last judgment in God's presence. At that time, there would be no lawyers and no way to hide the truth. We will all be alone."

This is what raced through his mind as he walked out in the balmy Boston night. His fate was in the hands of two U.S. federal agents with the vast powers of the government at their disposal, but this was no time to succumb to fear. In fact, he felt a new strength, even a sense of bravado, invade his consciousness: "If my son could survive, why not me?" he asked himself.

He chose not to make any phone calls. His destiny would have to work itself out. There was no other option.

After the three men checked into their rooms and met at the restaurant, Lamin chose to unburden himself of the vague bloody images that had been running through his mind all day. He had been unable to shake off the picture of Aziz fallen on the bridge, the thick red blood he had donated so regularly to the Red Cross spilling wastefully on the gate to the plane. He thought of the bone marrow sample that was needled out of him to help his son Yussef. Aziz was not the sentimental type, but he did believe that donating blood was one of the few selfless human acts left. It was a gift with no expectations. We have monuments for unknown soldiers; maybe the time has come to do the same for anonymous blood donors. Whatever they do, they save lives without having to take any.

"I don't know how long this will take," Lamin started, "but I hope you know they shot the wrong guy."

"Why do you say this? How much did you know about his personal life?"

"As much as anyone could possibly know. You don't expect me to know everything about him, or even about my wife and son. Why, I hardly know enough about myself. I very often wonder where I came from."

"Morocco," said Mr. Santucci with a smile.

"It could as easily have been Corsica. Or Provence in France. Or whatever."

"Sure. Tell us what you knew about his business."

"Web solutions, he used to say. Invested in real estate. He owned a restaurant for a while. He was contemplating a limousine business. His mind never stopped thinking about new possibilities. America was saturated, to be sure, every inch taken over by some franchise or corporation. Yet people could still strike it rich producing *kefir*— you know, the East European dairy food, which tastes like a mix of yogurt and buttermilk. He saw business opportunities everywhere. Invested in Toyota. Trusted Buffett. That kind of thing. We talked endlessly about his plans. Not mine, mind you. That exasperated him."

"Why?"

"He had no time for academics. Didn't get it. We appeared to him as helplessly self-absorbed nerds still stuck in the classroom's front row. Not that I ever sat in one, but that's how he saw it."

"What kind of education did he have?"

"Archaeology. He was fascinated by the Roman legacy, but the Graduate Center in New York didn't offer the courses he wanted. Plus, there is no Rome in New York and the subject seemed oddly out of place in the city. New York brought out his entrepreneurial instincts. When he first rode up to the top of the World Trade Center, he looked down on the city and dreamt of riches, not knowledge. He was so mesmerized by America's possibilities that he could easily have been lifted into thin air. Money drove him, but he never lost interest in ideas, culture. He was—is—was, I guess—one of the most intelligent people I have ever met. He was also very quick with languages. His English was impeccable."

It felt painful to for Lamin to be talking about his friend in the past tense, as if part of him had also died. They had drinks the day before, as he was telling him about his planned getaway to Oaxaca on Aeromexico. What better gift to Linda than a week in her native state? That way, the baby in her belly would be exposed to the air, food, and sounds of her ancestral land. She had gotten used to her husband not sharing his plans until the last minute. She probably had no clue they were leaving to Mexico until they got to Logan earlier on the same day Lamin drove down.

The FBI men asked Lamin about their own trips to Morocco and New York City. There was nothing striking about these excursions, except if he were to recount the endless times they built business empires on napkins and shook hands over drinks in bars, as if merely doing so and no more were enough to lift their spirits and give meaning to their American lives. They always walked out of the bars chastened, ready to resume their old lives, not embark on new adventures. As much as they liked taking risks, they were also aware of the passing of time. It had always been so, even in their separate childhood days in Tangier.

By the end of dinner, they had covered the few loose ends of Aziz's American life—the kinds of things that left no traces anywhere, activities that required no credit card transactions, or official paper work that could be stored somewhere. Lamin even had the uncanny feeling that the FBI men knew more about his friend's life in America than he did. The arm of the law was longer than the hand of friendship.

They moved to the lounge and settled in more comfortable chairs around a small table with a bright rose in a long, skinny vase. Lamin thought of blood some more. He ordered red wine Mr. Blanchard asked for cranberry juice and Mr. Santucci requested diet coke. Lamin managed to smile at the irony.

"You're sure you are not Muslim?" Lamin asked. "No

beer or wine. Nothing?"

They cracked a friendly smile and said something about work and regulations.

"Coke has always been my favorite drink," Lamin commented. "When I was a teenager, I kept it by my bed, in case I got thirsty in the middle of the night. I already told you I don't like water."

The men didn't know where their person of interest was going with his but, feeling pressured, he quickly knew what to say next. He looked at Mr. Santucci and asked him if he knew that Coca-Cola owes its existence to a nineteenth-century Corsican chemist and winemaker who was the first European to mix wine with coca leaves. This got both men's attention.

"His name is easy to remember—Mariani. His wine was quite popular among rich Europeans. Artists and scientists, including Edison, used it for energy. A pope was addicted. It inspired John Pemberton to do the same in this country. One day, he took out the alcohol and kept the rest, mostly for medicinal purposes. Then, he extracted the cocaine from the beverage and, voila!— wholesome, family-friendly Coca-Cola is born. You see, it all goes back to Mariani, to Corsica. What would this country be without Coke, without Mariani? Corisca gave us Napoleon and the idea for coke. Not bad, I'd say."

Mr. Santucci smiled while Mr. Blanchard displayed no discernible expression.

Lamin had said enough, he thought. After their drinks had been served, his mind and body were sufficiently composed and aligned and his fatigue largely lifted. He was comfortable enough to sink into a long meditative trance and tell them about his story with Aziz.

It turned out that talking to the FBI was far from the

worst ordeal that would afflict Lamin. He got in touch with Aziz's mother La Batul in the district of Souani where his mother lived with Aziz's three sisters. He talked to her every single day, sometimes more than once. He cried with her on the phone. He retold the story to her daughters. He emailed them in English, which they understood, or, if not, translated into French through one of Google's language tools. He communicated every piece of information conveyed to him by federal officials. He clipped newspaper articles; forwarded anything he could find online; and directed them to news accounts in French, Spanish, and Arabic, for which they didn't need his translation. He did this furiously during the first week, when Aziz's death was still major news, before new events relegated his friend, in a single blow, literally overnight, to the dungeons of historical trivia, the wasteland of collateral damage. One week and the story was done, folded. The headlines were long gone, but not a page in national newspapers had space for the tragic incident that consumed Lamin and the Nejjar family. Other deaths had to be accounted for, other news. And so he woke up one day to a second death, a scriptural and visual erasure as abrupt as his friend's violent entry into the world's consciousness. Then came the harder part.

One would have thought that La Batul would be prepared by the time Lamin arrived two weeks later. The facts were easy to forward, but how does one translate the mood of press releases, official reports, and public statements? How does one convey the professional tone of all-business officials who describe the death of Aziz in such a matter-of-fact manner that one forgets for a moment whether the victim is a human being or a broken car? No American official cried over the death of an innocent man. Death in America appeared as a mere accident in the endless search for hidden threats, the dogged pursuit of ghosts in a well-lit place. She understood how one might die for being in the wrong place at the wrong time. Tragedy happens. But understanding didn't diminish the shock of alienation. People cry when they kill the wrong person; they prostrate themselves in front of the victim's kin and seek mercy; they flagellate themselves to rid themselves of the horror that would haunt them for the rest of their lives; they even end their lives to atone for the crime of murder, a sin so enormous that it cannot be washed away, unless the victim himself exonerates you. The victims themselves.

But all Lamin had were more bloodless reports pulled out of the right folder. A suspicious Middle Eastern-looking individual was shot by an air marshal on 07/16/06 at 13 hours and 17 minutes. Like that. Death is spun out of any content, emptied out of its sacred meaning. Even a barely literate woman like La Batul could feel that, as distant as she was in Tangier. The blood of her Arab and Berber ancestors ran through her soul like an energizing force. The same blood that was negligently spilled in Boston. She was from a place where people speak a different language and have a store of emotions that was spiced up by the bitter heat of history, the warmth of the Mediterranean and African suns, and the bounties of land and sea. She lived on the debris of ancient powers that came seeking possessions or to satisfy insatiable appetites, and then vanished back into the ocean. At least the Phoenicians, Romans, Portuguese, and even the Spaniards built walls that withstood the fury of the *sharqi* winds. Different masters, they were. Not like the new ones who so mesmerized her son with their kaleidoscopic colors. This new power is here and there at once, one that saves and kills, neither present nor absent; it was like some addiction that found its way to the heart of nations through strange foods like Coca-Cola and chewing gum. America connects the world through its endless array of products—who can know anything today without Google's brain power?—only to disappoint it later through its unfiltered chauvinism.

La Batul saw many Americans on television, but she was never sure who among the thousands of tourists who walked through the city actually were.

"May God help us if we all became American without knowing it! No, no, that can't be. Aziz's beautiful wife is not really American. She has no blue eyes. Hers are as black as mine. A *spañola*, Spanish girl lost in America—just like my son was. Whatever they call them over there. Mexican. Latina."

"Yes, La Batul, and I can't wait to see her baby. She is six months pregnant now."

La Batul wiped a tear.

"That granddaughter—it's a girl, right?— is my only hope. You, too, my boy, and your son Yussef, may God protect him. I hope Linda comes to live here, in Tangier. And your wife, too, may God guide her. All of you. This is your place, right here."

"I hope so, too."

I knew that Aziz had left enough money to support his mother, wife, and child for a lifetime.

"The emotion was getting too intense for me," Lamin recounted as he moved uncomfortably in his chair in Cafe Smara. "I was made to stand for something that wasn't me—or was it? The Nejjars' grief had turned into a sort of menace, as if I had something to do with what happened. I had lost a friend, too, and was as aggrieved as anybody else. Not that I am contesting the primacy of blood—blood speaks louder than words and guns—but

Aziz was part of my life. We found our way separately to America and we both had plans to make some kind of difference in our own manner. He landed on the New World with the appetite of a mogul, while I dedicated my life to reading and writing. I knew the power of scripts. He knew the power of business. I taught literature and composition, while he built real and virtual networks. He made money. Just when he thought he was reaching the top, the American furies rose to claim his life."

A gentle breeze blew into the Nejjars' house through the window and brought the family back to its senses. Hardened expressions gradually dissolved into soft flabby faces, as if one moment had been condensed into five decades. Lamin saw a glimpse of old age, the sorrow of a lifetime. He saw the indelible marks of violence, the enigma of being alive in a world that we can't control. More hugs ensued. La Batul pulled him to her, held his head in her hand, and kissed his forehead. When she released him, she just stood in the living room, frozen, confused, lost.

It was time for Lamin to walk out. Instead of strolling to Cafe Smara, he walked toward Cafe Hanafta, the bamboo-sheltered open cafe on the eucalyptus shaded park overlooking the ocean, drawn to the scene by the urge to sit cross legged on the floor and listen to men playing Andalusian music out of sheer love for beauty. The *kif* fumes emanating from the pipes around him were diluted by the ocean breeze. The perfumed air that blanketed the scene had such a calming effect on his edgy nerves that he stretched out on the reed mat on which most of the men sat. Someone wrapped a *jellaba*, the universal all-purpose Moroccan gown, and put it under his head. Within minutes, he fell asleep. The voice of men singing, interrupted by the *mueddin*'s call for the sunset prayer, showered him with the feeling that life, at that moment, in that out-of-the-way place in Tangier, away from big hotels, airports, and boulevards, still preserved something of what had long been lost. Lost to whom or what? The sleep did him much good.

When he left the cafe, he chose to go to a new bar, instead of his family house. It was too early for him to sleep—the jet lag didn't help—and too late to join his mother for dinner. The place looked deliberately dark, with the men all seated around the counter sipping their beers and picking at their tapas. He sat at a table not too far from the counter. He didn't know what to drink, so he ordered the same Flag Special everyone was drinking. The beer came with marinated olives; he ordered a second, and it came with tiny grilled sardines; then a third with bits of kefta.

Not long after he took his first sip, someone tapped him on the back. It was his high school friend Zakaria. He stood up and they hugged, talked, and then sat down. Zakaria was doing well in some foreign subsidiary, although he had yet to find a wife and start a family.

"Any children?" Zakaria asked.

"Yes, a boy. Yussef. He just turned eight."

"Happy birthday! It's a great age. May he live to one hundred and ten!"

Obviously, Zakaria didn't know about Yussef's struggle with death. So they talked about Aziz.

"How are you doing with all that noise? To be in the middle of such an international mess. This must weigh on you."

"It is beginning to, but not too much to give up."

"I see. So what do you think?"

"Think? Many things. Feel? That's a different matter."

"Right."

"I am just shocked. But then I am familiar with death. Some of my neighborhood friends died when they were still children. I saw people drown. I lived with people on the verge of death."

"Yes, but this is different. Aziz was shot seven times."

"I know, but I wasn't there to see it. And by the time I went to the gate where all this happened, I saw nothing. Turned out that Aziz died on a gangplank, literally nowhere, neither land nor sky. Not even on a plane. A movable bridge, a tube. The place he died on might now be in a junkyard, for all I know. Or perhaps already broken down into its metal components for recycling. I didn't know where to put the bouquet of flowers I had taken with me to the site the following day. I couldn't leave it by the gate. It's against security rules. I just gave it to an airline worker."

Zakaria shook his head in amazement.

"To this day, I have never seen someone shot to death in real life. Or just someone shooting a gun, period. It's all like a movie. I had seen people use knives when I lived here, but I never saw a real person shooting a gun."

"Quite a traumatic experience."

"Yes, it is. Things get more complicated in my mind by the hour. I don't think straight anymore."

"How so?"

"Aziz is dead—that we know. But the rest is confusing. Take, for example, the outrage by Arabs and Muslims. They are using Aziz to complain about American imperialism. OK, but Aziz didn't like these people at all. Not that he was crazy about the American way of life, but Aziz was happier with Americans than he would be with such people. Many of these Arabs and Muslims would have shunned him, perhaps even stoned him if they had known him. And what do you think those Al Qaeda types would do to us if they saw us right now? Here in Tangier, Morocco, an Arab and Muslim nation? It's already tough enough as it is having to endure the cheap moralism of the average guy, but seeing it on a global scale is tougher. I mean, people tell me that Aziz is a *shaheed*, a martyr, in the eyes of God. Give me a break! A martyr? He's a victim. And whose God are these guys talking about, anyway? He certainly didn't share theirs. Really! What would you do if La Batul remembered her son as a good Muslim? You just listen, right? It's hard dealing with American law enforcement agencies and the American media's half-educated guesses about Morocco. Stereotypes run deep. They are a pain to immigrants like me."

"They think we are all Talibans, or a mixture of Sunni and Shiite clans, right?"

"Basically, and why would you expect them to know more? We also have no clue about them, except what television shows us. Mostly fantasies of America, not the dreadful drudgery of everyday life."

"That may be true, but there's a difference, though. They still rule the world, and anyone who rules anything must at least have an idea about what they are ruling. We have no control; they do."

"Maybe. You have a point there, but still. My point is I will leave in a few days, but you will have to hide in bars like these to have a drink. It's like a Moroccan kind of Muslims Anonymous. The secret society of drinkers."

"I drink anywhere I want," retorted Zakaria. "On the cafe-terraces of the beach during summer. In my home. I defy anyone to challenge me."

Lamin laughed. Zakaria was born a redoubtable debater. Nobody could win an argument with him. He'd use anything at his disposal to silence his opponents. He was tough.

"The way I see it," Zakaria continued over another beer, "is that this country is at a crossroads. The *beards* on one side, and drunks on the other."

Zakaria paused and smiled.

"OK, I am exaggerating a bit, but you get the point."

"Who do you think will prevail?"

"OK, the half-drunks. Beer, wine, or Andalusian music, it doesn't matter. No one can turn this place into Afghanistan. This is not some rugged wasteland. This is Tangier, Morocco. This is the legacy of Al-Andalus. Pleasure is encoded in our genes. We are almost Spanish. I raise my glass to the good life."

"Here's to Tangier."

Lamin spent the following day helping La Batul and the Nejjars set up for the Quran reciters, the *tulba* event. Around six o'clock in the evening, just after the sunset prayers, fifteen men with *jellabas* arrived and took their seat on the divans lining the walls of the living room. The guests sat in adjoining rooms, or wherever else they could, while tea and desserts were being served. Then in the same tone used to pray for the dead in cemeteries, the *tulba* started reciting the Quran while looking around them and even conversing through facial signs and hand gestures. The recital could not be interrupted, unless it was for the food that would be served later, or for the prayers offered for the dead, his family, and everyone in that house. Aziz would have been out of place in this setting, but he had no control now, even though he was buried in an old Congregational cemetery near his home in Connecticut.

"When we die," Lamin reflected, "our cultures claim

us back, against our will, if necessary. The verses about death and redemption were poignant; those about unbelievers, the *kuffar*, too. Their day of reckoning is coming. Their triumph is illusory but their punishment will be long lasting."

By eleven o'clock, the Nejjars wrapped up and Lamin left directly to his house. The only stop he made was at an Internet cafe on the way. He checked his email and the magazine he edited online. Things were otherwise quiet at home. His wife Jen and son Yussef were fine.

Not many guys from Cafe Smara attended the *tulba* recital, but Lamin got to see most of them the following day. The environment seemed uncharacteristically quiet, almost funereal. He was the middle man in a swirling saga of violence, trying to connect what could not be connected. But he was the man to talk to. He had access to both sides. Larbi, a policeman, started:

"How is La Batul doing?"

"Hanging in there."

"God help her," commented the waiter as he wiped my table and put my glass of unfiltered mint tea with reduced sugar.

"Amen," retorted Mamun, the cab driver.

"Add my voice to that," said Jebli, the smuggler.

"The good news is that his wife is expecting a girl."

"What happened to that boy? Don't they have condoms in America?"

"Come on," Jebli scolded Mamum. "This is not the time for profanities. Keep your mouth shut."

"Well?" Larbi asked again.

"Well, there isn't much you don't know. Aziz is another casualty of the war on terror. We don't get to choose our casualties. They just drop dead."

The men at other tables had come closer now. Even

the cafe owner and full-time employee at a local bank, Si Merzouk, found a strategic place to sit. Then he fired the question on everyone's mind:

"Won't they shoot all Arabs and Muslims eventually?"

"I don't know."

"Isn't being a Muslim or Arab these days like being a terrorist or a madman?"

"It's hard to avoid that feeling, but actually it's not quite like that. People don't treat me as one, although I am not sure what they think. Maybe they think all Muslims are in sleeper cells."

The faces were hardening again. The heat was rising. Those inscrutable looks, a blend of pain and threat, were once again on Lamin. At that instant, all those men could have come out of *The Good, the Bad, and the Ugly* or *Once Upon a Time in the West*. Those immovable faces scarred by wild errands and restless lives. The lack of a steady place. The absence of civilization. The law of the mighty.

Just as Lamin was trying to figure out how to handle this session—and he had been doing nothing but answering questions and commenting on the East/West divide since Aziz's death—Pedro and Amran walked in.

"That's all I needed," Lamin thought. "A Christian and a Jew to add to my problems."

Both men were Moroccan, although Pedro had a Spanish passport and Amran had French papers. They could leave the country for good any time they wanted, but both had long told their children, all of whom had settled across the world, that they were going nowhere. This was their home.

Lamin stood up as and they made their way through the tightly arranged chairs to hug him. Amran didn't mince his words.

"Good to see you, son. But don't even think of staying. I know things are hard for you over there. But there is nothing for you here. Look around."

Mamun, not known for his social graces, shouted back:

"Better than any Jewish place you'd find."

Pedro intervened:

"Good to see you. Don't pay attention to these crazy squabbles."

Si Merzouk had squeezed a couple of chairs next to his and both men sat down. Within minutes, their favorite drinks were served.

This interlude helped Lamin laugh a little. There is something about the place that had a restorative effect on him. Maybe that's why Amran never left. Pedro— well, Pedro knew what's on the other side of the sea. He visited his children and siblings at least twice a year. But he always came back saying, "There's nothing for me over there." He made that pronouncement so nonchalantly that he offended many people over the years.

"How could you say that?" a young man once confronted him. "People die every day trying to reach Spain, and you are telling us there's nothing there? You watch Spanish television with us, don't you? Don't you think there's more there than we have over here? Why would mothers risk death if there wasn't anything there?"

Pedro answered such challenges with yet another typical response.

"That's my view. You are welcome to yours."

And with that he brought an end to whatever dispute was in the making, adding to the confusion that reigned everywhere south of Europe. Things had to be better in Spain, but Pedro was telling us they were not. Later, other Europeans would support Pedro, but these types never sat in cafes like ours. They couldn't speak our language.

They came for cheap housing in the sun. Some came for sex. Talk about new colonialism. We were economic and military partners, but the country was gradually being taken over by a new army of settlers. *Pieds blancs*, I guess. This was the invasion of the European rich fleeing blandness and the retired extending the value of their pensions. The land was getting more expensive by the day. The food was also out of reach for millions. People were now truly homeless. No visas to work in Europe and no way to raise a decent family at home. But these new European settlers, who come and go as they please, don't like extremism. They get unsettled by the dark looks of bearded men and the covered bodies of hot, honey-colored women. They want to meet happy Moroccans with fancy homes and disposable incomes.

Larbi brought them back to the subject.

"So how did they treat you?"

"You mean security officials?"

"Yes."

"Reasonably well. The higher ups, like my FBI interrogators, were actually intelligent and sympathetic."

"They say that American police officers are not corrupt, they don't take bribes."

"Like you do," commented Jebli. "It's all one big mafia here."

"I am not sure," I replied. "American cops don't pocket bribes but they make money for their state or city. It's a business, an industry. They'd stop an Arab merely for looking like one. Like with the blacks and Mexicans."

"Or the Jews, if you are in Europe," added Farid.

"I'd agree with that," said Amran. "We are not out of the loop yet."

"How so? Jews are doing quite well. How long will you use that victim card?" Si Merzouk objected.

"You think?" asked Amran who was seated next to him. "Only the short-sighted think so. Hitler died in 1945. That's less than a century ago. A mere second in Jewish time. History grants us moments of reprieve, but it takes them back."

Lamin was stunned to hear this exchange. In all the years he had spent in the United States, he had never heard this perspective, expressed in such a manner. Living there, one got the impression that Jews and Christians were a happily married couple whose only problem was the Muslim, the dark Arab. The Judeo-Christian body was undivided; no scars of history were visible on its parts. He asked Amran if that was the real reason he chose to stay.

"Well, think. Better here than there, like Pedro says. These are my roots. Why change them for something that won't last."

This was even more stunning to his Americanized sensibilities.

"Won't last?"

"Nothing's forever," commented Farid to everyone's relief. "It all evens out in the end. Here or there, it doesn't really matter. Jewish or Muslim. Or Spaniard."

"Yes, but don't the extremists attack Jews and Christians. We call them extremists, but they are the brainwashed fools of Saudi Arabia, the dumbest nation on the planet."

"You mean that Wahhabi stuff," Larbi clarified.

"Yes. The heavy-duty Sunni stuff."

"We are all Sunnis here."

"Whatever that means," interjected Merdi.

"And what does that mean?" asked Pedro.

"I am not sure myself. The Sunnis think the Shiites are the Jews and Christians' cousins. Unbelievers. *Kuffar*.

So they kill them and blow up their sacred shrines. If this is what the Sunnis do, I want nothing to do with them. The Sunnis are disgracing my religion."

"Bravo," applauded Mamun. "I am a cab driver, so I never get this shit—excuse my language. I never heard of this stuff till the Americans broke up Iraq. Now it's all over the place. I even have foreign customers who ask me if I am Sunni or Shiite. What do I care? I'd rather be in bed with a blonde, and let me die a Jew."

"The *beards* are the best smugglers I know," commented Jebli. "They aren't more virtuous than I am."

"Anybody is more virtuous than you," replied Mamun.

"I wish I could tape you guys and take this back with me to the States." Lamin said wistfully. "People don't talk like this over there. It's all muted and dangerous. America is like Iraq—red lines everywhere."

"Too bad," commented Si Merzouk. "In my cafe, everything goes. We are an open society here. Smart people. We may not have university degrees, but we think. I watch good TV programs. You may have noticed that I have the only cafe in town that doesn't have Al Jazeera on all day long. If you want to watch Al Jazeera, go to the cafe next door. Here we stick to our Spanish channels. We watch Moroccan TV only when our king speaks to us or if there is a good soccer game on. That's it."

"Cafes now have two TV sets on," explained Farid, "one for Al Jazeera and the other for all the other channels."

Larbi once again intervened.

"How do we manage to get off track. Let Lamin finish his story."

"What do you want to know?"

"We were talking about the cops."

"I told you. They are cut from the same general cloth.

They have the same prejudices. The same virtues."

"What else?"

"That's it—just don't mess with them. It's the same here, everywhere."

"That's right."

More men gathered, including a few with long, well-groomed beards. America was everywhere in the news and here was Lamin, one of them, coming back to report on it. They were curious about the Arabs' new enemy. The French, our old colonizers, now looked good—almost angelic, Lamin thought. Even their tough-talking president Sarkozy sounded reasonable, almost like a friend. The Europeans were, for better or worse, mixed up with Morocco. They fought us; they married us; they appointed the children of our immigrants to ministerial posts. Sarkozy's wife had an affair with a Moroccan. We should have guessed that when she later divorced him, he would go for an Italian model. I guess Braudel was right: we all breathe the air of the Mediterranean. But Americans were somehow different. They were new to us, an abrupt appearance, like the Vandals. They swept through the land like a hurricane, wiping out anything that stood on their way, until they marched their way out of history. They kept going till they could go no more.

"It's hard to be a translator," Lamin said. "You are definitely bound to betray. I don't even know myself that well, but I was now required to explain enemy nations to each other. Forget Islam—how does one explain America when everyone is touched by it? There was Aziz's wife, too, and she also needed to be explained correctly, not to be mixed up with other Americans. She had her own story to tell, her own store of woes and tragedies. Like Aziz, she was neither here nor there, but she felt the strong pull of Arab blood in her veins. There was not a trace of Anglo blood in her. No ancestors from the British Isles or Northern Europe. No Protestants. It's all dark and Latin."

La Batul was right; America is like a veiled woman, seen and unseen at once. Bashir once told his son that American women were too much for him. He'd rather be with European women inspired by Hollywood; that way you got two in one. Classic European flesh retouched by Hollywood. I know what he meant. Perhaps this was a lesson that Aziz took to heart. People are more American when they are not. Real Americans do things their way, but other people imagine their own America. It's like a fantasy that people won't outgrow. A permanent state of adolescence. Then real Americans show up with guns and ruin the dream. This is what makes people mad. Americans are not supposed to be *that* bad. Mischievous like Blondie, maybe, but not vicious.

All the men in the cafe were over fifty. They had known a different time, when the city was a pleasant refuge for all lifestyles. American and European writers came to live and play. Others came to hide. Some men in the cafe, like Ahmed, had indulged in the pleasures of the city before they cleaned up their lives, married, had children, and went on pilgrimage to Mecca. They came back as *hujjaj*. One *hajj*, Ahmed Medwi, told Lamin that he had had enough of life once he had performed the ritual. "I am just doing time," he added with a beatific smile.

Maybe more Muslims are doing time. The old and the young. The *hujjaj* and the martyrs; the men in bars and the men in cafes; the women at home and the prostitutes in nightclubs; the cops and the human bombs. Come to think of it, maybe we are all—Muslims and non-Muslim— doing time. We are all waiting for our purification rituals before we call it quits. I don't know. This whole story got me too depressed. Lamin hadn't been able to sleep since Linda called him on his cell phone that July afternoon with the news. He had yet to make sense of the death. He didn't even write an article in his magazine about it. He knew his readers had been waiting, but he was just too exhausted.

Lamin was suddenly allowed to say things a little bit his way. On top of the loss, fatigue, and endless rounds of talks with family and friends, and interviews with officials, he hadn't been able to say much himself. People would ask him but then would insist on bending his account to suit their beliefs. He was becoming a cipher, not a witness whose opinion was sought. No sooner would he start answering a question than someone would interject with a comment to steer the discussion in the direction he wanted. But Lamin didn't want to leave Tangier without checking out what people were really thinking. His cafe buddies were not the sheepish type. They had studied the world from its edges. They knew a con when they saw one.

"I am not exactly sure who is to blame here," he finally got himself to say.

"What do you mean?" asked Merdi.

"Well, I mean would Aziz have died if the Muslims, his so-called brothers, hadn't provoked the tiger?"

"You mean the terrorists?"

"Yes."

"Good question. And I don't give a damn about the CIA baloney. You don't shoot at a tiger and run away. You invite destruction. Death."

"But they shoot at us, too," protested Mamun.

"They can do that. Time is on their side. That's how it goes. The mighty devour the weak," replied Merdi.

"What about democracy, then?"

"Never believed in it. A nice dream. It'll always be the law of the jungle till the jungle is burnt up."

"The terrorists didn't have to go all the way over there to seek justice. One could do a good deed right here, in this cafe, and get better rewards. What did they do? They killed a bunch of people in those buildings."

"Are you sure they did?"

"They are doing it over here, over there in Madrid. They almost killed my niece on that train. They bombed Casa de España and a synagogue in Casablanca. How would you like it if some *beard* stabbed Amran here and killed him. What would that do for Allah? Now tell me."

Lamin could see the religious types a bit unsettled.

"What I couldn't understand," Pedro jumped in, "is that guy from Tangier. What's his name? Jamal? Looks like a nice guy. What led him into the hands of those mad people in Madrid?"

"Loneliness," said Mamun. "Lack of sex. I am not kidding you. We sleep with the tourists or kill them. Our bodies are bursting with repression. We don't even know how to enjoy women. I mean, here I am, with this Italian lady—in her fifties—and she blew my mind away. I never knew so much pleasure was possible."

"Show some respect," enjoined Ahmed.

"Respect! I have been hearing that all my life. I never gave a damn. Talk about the Saudis and their Wahhabi stuff. I have driven so many girls to their palaces. And these guys are married. With children. How do you explain that?"

Hesitation.

"When they were kids, they had no place to put their dicks in. So they sought anything that moved. We do it here, too. But here we have bars, nightclubs, prostitutes, widows . . . you know what I mean. That's why all the

Bedouins are here. What do you think? They don't build palaces in Afghanistan! The custodians of the Ka`aba prefer Tangier. Now, you tell me why."

That's how Mamun always spoke. But at least he expressed something Aziz and Lamin believed. No one took up his question.

"Look, guys," Ahmed broke the silence again, "call me a dinosaur, if you want, but this business of attacking Arabs and Muslims won't do us any good."

"Why not?" asked Merdi.

"Because it weakens our ranks and resolve."

"We never had any, don't you get it? Look here: Algeria chasing Morocco in the Sahara, Iraqis slaughtering themselves, the Sunnis bombing the Shiites, the ayatollahs and the Taliban cavemen harassing their women, the Lebanese bombing each other, Muslims killing Christians in Egypt and Lebanon, the Turks obsessed with the Kurds, the Palestinians seeking the mediation of the Saudis, Yemenis bombing Spanish tourists. It never stops. If this weren't enough for you, look at your own history. We never allowed those Ottomans here, never mind their nonsense talk about the caliphate. Our sultans made sure they didn't take our country. The funny thing is I was once in Turkey and they had this map of the Ottomans that included Tangier. That shows you how power hungry the Turks are. In the name of Islam. Let me take over, then, if you don't care which Muslim holds power. Me, I'd chose a Spaniard over an Ottoman anytime. This damn Pedro may have my blood for all I know; the Ottomans are Asian, Mongols."

"Good," a man chimed in. "Muslims bombing Muslims everywhere in the name of Islam. Too much. I'd rather smoke my *kif* and listen to music. To hell with the fanatics."

The discussion was a relief, but it was far from what Lamin needed to sort out his thoughts. He needed a sounding board. He wanted good advice. But he was leaving in a day and a half. He would have loved to stay in the sunny weather that shrouded the city, but work and family called him back. This trip was a good end to an emotional roller coaster. Moroccans didn't want to know about Aziz as much as Americans did. He walked down to Liberty Avenue, a small winding street connecting old Tangier to the new, the one built by the French and Spanish. It was on this street that Amran's tailor shop was located. It had been there since he was born and since his father was a child. As far as he knew, it had always been there, at least since Perdicaris built himself a mansion there and married the English woman he seduced in London. Who remembers now that the rich seducer would end up being kidnapped by the first modern jihadist, Raisuli, and that Teddy Roosevelt would use the occasion to threaten retaliation against the Muslim terrorist? But Raisuli was no Bin Laden, Perdicaris was no American citizen, Teddy was no Bush, and the story had a somewhat happier ending.

It almost felt like Amran had been expecting him. He shook his hand and tapped him on the back and head, much like he did when he was a child. He was the one who told his father to teach Lamin foreign languages. He had wanted the boy to go the Jewish school in town, like many of his friends did, but his father thought it was too long a walk from home and chose to sign him up at the public school, Tarik ibn Ziyad, instead. Lamin did develop a fondness for English and Spanish, although French, the language spoken everywhere in the country, didn't somehow suit his mood. English was plain and square; Spanish felt dramatic and even tragic; but French was too poetic and full of literary turns for a young boy to appreciate. French was also unavoidable in our schools, but English and Spanish were matters of choice then. Things are different today. Who can avoid English now?

"Exactly," affirmed Amran. "This is the hour of English. Languages have their time in the sun, too. It's not just nations and religions. Never mind this: Tell me, what brings you here? I know you want to see me; I can tell something is bothering you. You looked ill at ease in the cafe yesterday. What happened to Aziz is not easy. My wife Biba and I were the first to hear about the news and console La Batul. Although she lacks for nothing, we offered to help with the *tulba*. Yet I know this is not the only thing that is bothering you. What is it?"

"I am leaving tomorrow, Si Amran, but I haven't been able to think clearly about this mess. I feel pushed around by the authorities and the public. No one has asked me to sit down, relax, and just say what I know and think. Everywhere I go, I feel that people want to extract the information they want from me. They are looking for clues that suit them. No one seems to be interested in anything beyond that."

"You mean Americans want information that makes them look right and righteous, and Muslims want the same."

"Exactly. But even this is not as simple as it sounds. The American government wants information that supports its foreign policy; American liberals want information that discredits their government; others want information that shows that all Muslims are terrorists or potential terrorists. It's only one man, Si Amran—one dead man—and many explanations."

"How about the Muslims."

"They, too, want to see everything through the lenses of the victim. To them, Aziz's death is clear proof that America is a ruthless assassin bent on killing all Muslims. They may know nothing about America, but try shaking them out of this view. Hopeless."

"That's how it is."

"I don't know how to tell Aziz's story. The problem is once you begin, the tale unfolds back into history until it vanishes in the mist of time. I mean, in the end we are talking about the ancient wars of Muslims and Christians, East and West, aren't we?"

"Well, yes, that's why Jews can't stop fighting anti-Semitism. It began a long time ago, but it hasn't stopped now. The struggle never ends."

"Muslims ought to be the allies of the Jews in this; instead they are fighting each other over land that is no bigger than the province of Tangier."

"These are difficult times, but they are getting better, even if they look worse. Things will work out when everybody is exhausted. It may be too late for me—or even you—to witness.

"I hope not. I just can't say things my way. And when I think I do, people take my words and turn them into something they want."

Si Amran wasn't that interested in these semantic dilemmas, so he brought up weightier matters.

"By the way, how is your son? We prayed for him, you know. The entire synagogue did."

"Thank you for asking, Si Amran. He is doing well. It wasn't easy to come out of that experience only to find myself dealing with the unexpected death of Aziz. Yussef's trial had renewed my faith in the world. I had so much hope. Then I was struck by Aziz's death. You win some and you lose some, I guess."

"We will continue to pray for Yussef and Aziz. Give our love to Linda and tell her that we are here if she ever needed anything."

After a long hug—the kind that could be the last one—Lamin walked one more time around the city before he went back to sleep and fly out to Newark in New Jersey via Paris. The great establishments of his youth had deteriorated beyond repair. Cinema Capitol made way for a cheap new building, Cinema Alcazar lay in ruins, Cinema America turned into a cafe, and the great Teatro Cervantes was on the verge of collapse. Satellite dishes and Internet cafes had sprouted everywhere, as did big-chain supermarkets. Gulf Arabs were buying up the whole city to turn it into one vast playground for the rich. The city needed an injection of money; it was getting it all right. The teachers, nurses, and waiters, not to mention the dying breed of librarians, kept being pushed to the edges of town. The culture of old Tangier had been replaced with information—Al Jazeera shouting in the face of MSNBC; Canal + competing with SkyTV. With the borders closed, young men had fewer places to seek relief—the mosque or late-night porno channels. Dozens of them. A new modernity had come to town, but it left the city breathless.

Lamin flew out of town the same way he came in. Confused. But he was relieved to be going back to the orderly world of Madison and university life. With Aziz gone, he could now give all his time to reading, writing, teaching, spending more time with Jen, and watching his son grow. He hoped to find safety in the American middle-class existence and leave his tumultuous life behind him.

OLD WORLD

From this point on, the story of Lamin is better known, at least among those who follow the doings in his academic field. He would bury himself in his basement to emerge a few years later with a book, then do interviews or write articles, and then he would go back again to his underworld of delights, digging deeper into the wells of history, crawling into the dark tunnels that lead to new worlds, even while he joined the denizens of the World Wide Web, surfing, emailing, and googling. For a while, he turned into an apostle of Open Source, championing projects like Wikipedia, authored by tens of thousands of anonymous hands, and embraced the high-speed powers of the Internet, traveling fast to distant realms without having to leave his house in Madison. But he knew that, ultimately, he relied on printed books and blood-and-flesh humans to stay alive. And when the two worlds of books and people are fused together the result can be shattering, as happened to Lamin when, at the age of fifty-five, he was taken aback by the sight of a woman who seemed to have walked out of some celestial realm into the dark interior surrounding the massive bronze crypt in the Cathedral of Seville. Her face was so brightly lit that it appeared engulfed in her own special aura, provoking in him a sensation that was a mix of thrill and awe. She was, he could swear, the exact embodiment of his dream woman, the one he imagined every afternoon when he was a teenager watching Spanish television during his naptime in Tangier—long black hair like grace descending straight from heaven, black piercing eyes that see through you all the way back to the Garden of the Hesperides, skin that seemed to have been crafted by the queen bees of Yemen, a gentle sweet smile that strikes like lightning, and a kind of intelligence that is neither cerebral nor bookish but nurtured by a knowledge beyond the reach of mere mortals. He felt that she had been sent to him and he didn't hesitate to speak first.

"Excuse me," he started. "I was just wondering whether Columbus is, in the end, still alive?"

She stopped with a smile.

"I mean, he is dead," continued Lamin," and DNA tests prove that it's him inside that chest, but the Dominicans are not giving up their claim to his remains. You think he's buried in two places?"

"Well, that's the paradox of all migrants, isn't it? We end up living in two places, or more, even. You think death solves that problem? Not in his case," she said pointing at the tomb.

"Especially if the place is not one!"

"Ah, of course. The Muslim Giralda is the beacon of this Catholic cathedral. He is buried on ground zero of the clash of civilizations."

"I can't believe you are saying this. I am on my way to Villena to watch their fiesta of Moros and Cristianos. To me, the whole country is ground zero of that clash—and its promise for peace."

"Is this new information for you?"

"Yes, because I spent decades in America—the United States, not the Dominican Republic!—where my historical focus was distorted by much Anglo bias."

"I am sorry for you. I spent two years at Yale. That was enough for me. Americans are like the Chinese—they think they can buy cultures, import them like they do cars or wines. They have the best libraries, so much money, lots of rules, but no philosophy besides counting, the only one that makes sense for shopkeepers and buisness moguls. It's a country of checklists."

Lamin could maintain a conversation with anyone at any time, but this time he just stood there stunned, almost shaken, surrounded by churchgoers, pilgrims, and tourists, watching her radiant face, fearing she might crystallize in front of his eyes into an angel and get out of reach. He invited her for coffee and she accepted immediately, without feigning hesitation, so far ahead of the norm she was.

"I am, by the way, Teresa."

"Lamin."

She was definitely younger than him, much younger at the age of thirty, a fact for which he was, unexpectedly enough, very grateful, as the age difference added another layer of protection for him. As they had coffee, he told her about his project of looking into the subtle and subversive powers of art to keep a certain memory alive, in this case that of the never-ending battles between Christians and Muslims. To him, it was a long overdue return to the basics, the origins, going through a most circuitous detour, beginning in Oaxaca, the native state of Linda's parents, making his way back through various parts of Mexico, all the way to the ambiguous state of New Mexico, finding traces of Moorishness every step of the way, and he marveling at how defeat in history is also an ironic victory because didn't we know that the glorious Catholics of Spain ended up spreading Moorish art and design, just like the defeated Aztecs in Mexico remained alive in their food, and that to win and lose, in the larger scheme of things, are only variations on the theme of cycles, not progress?

It was along these lines that Lamin spoke to Teresa as they drank coffee that September afternoon and it was in that mode that they remained, she explaining to him that she had spent five years with a renowned French philosopher before he broke down one evening while drinking his Ricard and announced that he couldn't marry her because she was too perfect for him, too feminine, or something like that, forcing her to pack up her suitcase and leave Paris for Madrid, where she resumed her life as a freelance writer and a part-time staff member at the Casa Árabe. She was in Seville attending a conference on the three Abrahamic religions organized by the Three Cultures Foundation.

"I know you'd be asking yourself, how in the world does a woman like Teresa end up in such a situation?" Lamin asked rhetorically on the last day of our formal conversation at the cafe. He looked rested, even younger, with his blue blazer and clean-shaved face. In moments like these, I could give him another fifty years to live, another lifetime of reading, writing, and adventures but, then again, he'd take one look in the direction of the outside terrace, where the sun shone brightly, and you'd think he was done with this business, that he was here for the show—his own, mostly.

"I know. I know a gorgeous, model-type girl in New York who can't find a boyfriend, while another woman, short, chubby and, quite frankly, ugly, can't keep men away. Not fair."

The moment I said this I knew I had trivialized the conversation by citing such mundane examples. But Lamin was kind. He smiled and let the conversation cool down on its own. He took a sip from his mint tea and looked out again.

"The thing with Teresa is I felt that she was sent to remind me of something, a part of me I had lost, one that I had never taken with me to America."

"Like what? Funny, but because I grew up in Rabat, I don't have that kind of relationship with Spain you or my father does. Spain is closer to you than it is to us."

"That's how it was when we were children. We were the only ones watching Spanish TV. Like I say, Spain is in our blood. It's true. The reason I was going to Villena is because a Spanish guy, a *festero*, acting as a member of one of the Christian groups fighting and defeating the Moors, pointed to his skin and told Max Harris, a great scholar of folk music, that we are all Moors."

"I see."

"Teresa's last name, by the way, is Medina. Well, Jurado Medina because of the way Spaniards use their family names."

"How did that day end?"

"It didn't. After coffee, we walked, then ate, before we ended up in a music bar. By that time, we had moved from the world of ideas to a metaphysical one, speaking like mystics without feeling the least bit self-conscious about it, and as the music played and the volume of the collective cheer rose, we kept looking at each other, burning with the fire of incertitude yet deeply aware of the consequences of one *faux pas*, only one, so we talked and talked, until we grew too tired to keep our eyes open, then we walked out of the bar and asked a taxi to drop us at our respective hotels. The following morning, we took the same train to Madrid, before I rented a car and drove to Villena to spend a week with Khadija and her Spanish boyfriend because the only hotel in town was fully booked."

"Why Villena?"

"Because I wanted to get to the heart of the clash of civilizations, between the West and Islam. The whole clash is reenacted and resolved in a week. I could have gone to the more famous festival in Alcoy, but the Moors of Villena are led by none other than the Prophet Mohamed himself, a dark man with a turban called Mahoma in Spanish. He is actually not a local, but borrowed from a neighboring town for the occasion. The Spanish troops are inspired by Our Lady of the Virtues, the dark Virgin nicknamed La Morenica. After a week of battles, marches, and final conversion of the Moors in the main church, life resumes and the people of Villena start planning for the next fiesta. It never ends."

"Is this your key to some kind of solution?"

"Maybe. I haven't finished this project yet. I have been going to Spain since that September in 2015."

"Did you see Teresa again?"

"Yes, in Madrid, after my week in Villena. We spent two days talking, even spending hours standing in the Cervantes tapas bar in the downtown area, sometimes squeezed within packs of people, and yet we managed to stay focused, almost as if our lives depended on it."

"Focused on what?"

"Well, focused in the sense that we couldn't let go of the conversation. We were trying to define ourselves against some powerful Western intellectual dogma. We were not religious—that was a given. But after that, we didn't know quite how to fit in. The Enlightenment, with its cult of reason and exaggerated worship of science, was too cold for us. We both believed in the power of mystery, but one can't rationalize this power. I think Teresa is Epicurean in a distinctly Spanish way, while I carried the vices of the port of Tangier. The Spaniards, you know, are quite austere people—don't let the wine and *allegrias* fool you. They have the discipline of conquerors and imperialists. Don Quixote is, actually, an anti-Spaniard character.

I just listened at this point. I could have commented with some silly conversation-making question, but that would have sounded utterly fake and out of place. I waited.

"We talked about George Santanaya, José Ortega Y Casset and Miguel de Unamuno but, in the end, we realized that the best description we could use—at least one that has been articulated before—is what an enigmatic philosopher by the name of Fritz Mauthner called 'godless mysticism.' This was the only rational explanation for my experiences with the *faqih* in Bukhash-khash and my physician friend Mohamed who took me to his master in a Sufi order in Tetouan. I never told you about Mohamed; your father knows him well. He was the best in his class, but he thought physical medicine was only the first step in the healing process. In fact, your engineer father and I agree when it comes to the reality of these experiences. We often talk about them."

I lost him a bit here, again. We are from the same country but I can't keep up with him. Is it a generational thing? These kinds of experiences don't happen to me, yet then his experience with Teresa is only five years old. I was already a university student at the time. It wasn't that long ago.

"What did you do after the discussion?"

"I flew back to Newark and told my wife about Teresa."

"Everything?"

"No. I can't explain the encounter in the Cathedral. It was designed by some cosmic power. WASPs like Jen simply can't countenance these sorts of experiences. They are too otherworldly for their practical—square, I guess—mind."

"Are you talking about white people? Because that is one of my most confusing experiences in America, although it's not the same in the city. I am not sure how to relate on the basis of race."

"Did you notice how some white Americans want to pigeonhole you into some nonwhite category out of sincere sympathy?"

"Yes, of course. It's very annoying, and pathetic. These are some of the plainest and ugliest people who claim some progressive ideology to save me from their fellow racist Americans."

"They are often weak and below average, but they have their whiteness to make them feel good. It's a strange American play."

"The thing is I don't understand why they divide the world into whites and others. What is white, anyway?"

"Exactly. That's why I said WASP, not white Catholics, Jews, Italians, etc. It's an over-generalization. Some Protestants are capable of an emotional brutishness that is terrifying. That is their ultimate weapon. The Native Americans, Blacks, and Latinos are not equipped to handle it. These white people live and die by their ruthlessness—it's in their laws, habits, workplace, you name it. And Teresa and I thought that the Inquisitor in *The Brothers Karazamov* is a mean Christian! He won't hold a candle to the Protestant mind. Not a candle."

His life was not the same after Seville. Yussef had left home to study at a university just before he traveled to

Spain, so coming back to an empty nester's home only aggravated the sense of alienation he had been feeling during the years following the death of Aziz. If it hadn't been for Jake Uphill, he probably would have left earlier. They took long walks, traveled together to Mexico, and smoked cigars on his backyard bench. Jack had lived at a time when America, following World War II, was still in the making. Because of his experience in the State Department, Lamin got interested in the Cold War and American Communism, trying to understand this distant and exotic moment in American history when Communists had a bit of influence before the vigilantes of law and order, defenders of the American way, rose from the margins to ruin lives and futures, until the hapless comrades who dared think against the grain of American capitalism were wiped out from memory, abandoned to the fringes of academia, where Lamin found some of them, worn out and defeated. His interest in this subject grew to the point that he almost published a major article about it, but his thesis—that an undefined America works as a censoring device—had no takers.

"I'd rather work on the Moors in Spain. That kind of history is closer to my heart."

"But you were once in love with America and its history?"

"Yes, I was."

"What happened?"

"To put it simply, the country lost its nerve. I can't give you a reason. Don't forget that America is both a romantic idea and a hard reality. The funny thing is that I dreamt of an America portrayed by Italian artists who never settled in it. Italian-Americans like Francis Ford Coppola and Martin Scorcese did a great job giving us a taste, but Sergio Leone, with the help of Ennio

Moriccone's haunting scores, captured its troubled soul. I know Jen is puzzled by my obsession with the Man with No Name trilogy and *Once Upon a Time in the West*, but how can I stop? There was a degree of noble heroism in those stories—bandits killing for money and riding, unattached, into the sunset. Remember Tuco in *The Good, the Bad and the Ugly*? He was left in the cemetery with his hands tied and a pile of cash by his side—his part of the treasure. Where was he going with that? Build himself a little house on the prairie? Open a taverna in Mexico? And where was Blondie riding with his cash? Start a farming business in Missouri?"

"It's one of my favorite movies, too. But I never saw it this way."

"I could write a book about it. Tuco is also, by the way, the first Mexican archvillain in American art. Think of the dozens of crimes he is accused of, each state or territory with its own set of laws. But Blondie walks away with the same amount of cash, as innocent as a lamb. These are the archetypes at the heart of American life today. I see Blondie and Tuco everywhere—literally everywhere."

"You are giving me ideas now. This is really interesting."

"Take a look at *Once Upon a Time in the West*. A different cast this time, all gringos, with a gorgeous woman in their midst. That's a film about honor—when promises meant something. That is also a spirit that has vanished. Remember my experience at the New York gym? The men in this film would have understood. Not the gym manager. It's all paperwork. All legalese. They kill with fine print now."

The only person Lamin had to share his views openly was Jake. They were both outside the academic mainstream—with Jake retired and Lamin working in an increasingly hostile environment, where honor mattered less than one's race or gender and hiding behind clichés was more important than wrestling with ideas. Maybe he had spent too much time in academia, watching a special breed of people who lived in boxes, moving from one to the other, interrupting their routines with sweating sessions in the gym, seeking permanent health and life for their starved bodies, not knowing, as Lamin kept saying over and over again, not knowing that they had become one-dimensional stick figures in a gothic play, moving in tandem toward a new death. I could see his burrowed forehead and squinting eyes as he looked around him in Madison, as if he were in a horror movie, and trying hard, very hard to find comfort in the fact that Jen was his wife and she was not, *absolutely not*, one of them.

"These were maddening sessions, very frustrating. I was worried, concerned, confused, lost," Jen once told me. "One day I just screamed in his face: 'I am your wife, the woman you fell in love with, the sweet blonde with a radiant face. Remember?'"

And Lamin would give Jen a big hug, reassure her that he loved her even more, make passionate love in their now empty house, go out for dinner, take a daytrip to Manhattan, even a long weekend, to get away from the funereal suburban life of Madison, mingle with the people, hear their accents, smell the odors of foreign lands, watch films with subtitles and then come back to Madison, hoping to be rejuvenated for another cycle with the same stick figures eating their salads and yogurts at their desks, keeping their checklists, plotting strategies for self-advancement, keeping their thoughts to themselves, and denouncing social injustice. His love for Jen was deep, genuine and enduring, but with Yussef out of the house, her sweet and unobtrusive ways, her quiet movements, her long silent stretches of reading and grading, gave him an unsettling sensation of slow death. He had spent more than thirty-five years making things work for him, his family, his many communities, in America and Morocco, only to find himself alone, face-to-face with the dark, gray skies of success. It was almost as if he had spent thirty-five years partying and woke up to the debris all around him. He felt frighteningly alone, contemplating an uneventful life in his tidy house, walking out in an empty street, and driving to some shopping center just to do something. It didn't matter how hard Jen tried to console him, snap him out of his rut, cheer him up by sharing with him the obituaries of eccentric people, he remained unchanged, not, however, without a deep sense of loss. He had been aware of all the traps of immigration, but he hadn't expected America to run her course this fast.

"America is a vast continent of opportunity, but it's not a place, or a real nation, despite all the patriotic paraphernalia that blankets the landscape during holidays; it is still a land of people trying to belong, each and everyone of us. It's exhausting."

"Did you share your feelings with Jake?"

"A bit. We talked about America as an idea, which is true, but then that's all he has. I must show respect."

Jake had been Lamin's best colleague and friend for decades, even in retirement, then, one day, he collapsed in his kitchen, while reheating his cup of coffee, leaving him alone, with no one to share his broad reflections on history and culture. He struggled to feign interest in chit-chat conversations at work, but he felt increasingly alienated. He threw himself more intensely in his Moorish project, reading furiously and uninterruptedly until he got a chance to go back and read more books in

Madrid, and then reconnect with Teresa again.

"The more I thought about Spain, the more I realized its greatness, its significance to world history, and the clues it could offer to Muslims, on how to become modern and still be yourself, your Moroccan self. Spain became my middle ground, the passageway, connecting point; I don't know, it was a place of slow rebirth for me."

It dawned on me how close we were to Spain sitting on that spot, and I still wondered which part had to do with Teresa and which with Spanish history. I was about to ask the question when I realized that I knew the answer, that Teresa and Spain are one and the same, inseparable, soil and flesh, blood and rivers, all part of the same spirit, the mystery, the power. Emboldened, I just stated: "Teresa is Spain."

"Al-Andalus, yes. Her academic knowledge is nourished by the courage of conquistadors, the tragic outlook of gypsies, and the heart of mestizo Moroccans. A *mora*, pure *mora*. When we talk, we need little prefacing, not like when I am in America talking to a John Cunningham."

"A little prefacing?"

He smiled. "Yes, a little. There are still cultural gaps there; smaller ones. Even tiny."

"But not in the mystical connection?"

"No, because that is a different dimension of life, ethereal, not bound by nations and our petty concerns. It's a gift."

Lamin and Teresa would roam the streets of Madrid all day, avoiding obvious landmarks like the Retiro gardens or Puerta del Sol or the Prado museum, heading instead to the San Isidro area, and exploring nearby cemeteries, especially where foreigners are buried, telling stories of unfinished journeys, hints of self-exile, and those expats who left their gray skies and lives for the warmth of Spain. In the evening, they would head to Cinema Renoir in Calle de la Princesa and afterwards to dinner and drinks till past midnight.

In the end, they both knew that theirs was an impossible situation and they parted ways, grateful to the fate that brought them together, if only to remind Lamin of what he had been missing all those decades he was busy being a good academic, husband, and father. Now, in retrospect, Teresa felt like an emissary from another world, sent to remind him that a transition back to his Moroccan life was possible; she may even have been an angel preparing him for the death of his mother at the dawn of the fateful year of 2019.

"I got a call in the first day of the year that she had a stroke and was in the Red Crescent clinic. I flew out that night with Iberia, and the following day I was by her side. She couldn't talk but she smiled. Three days later, I took her home and it was while I held her that she chose to leave. Our house was full of people—family members, old friends, neighbors—all coming to say goodbye and escort her to the cemetery. By the end of the month, when I boarded the plane back to Newark, I knew I had been emptied out of whatever ambition and enthusiasm had motivated me to take off more than thirty-five years before. I was now flying to a new country. It was like going nowhere."

"The moment I landed I knew I was leaving, going back to Tangier. I didn't know how and when, but, in my heart of hearts, it was already a *fait accompli*. All I needed to do is convince Jen. Yussef was already away and he would have no problems joining us during his vacations."

But Jen, as we know now, couldn't take that leap. She loved her husband and wondered whether she could be like Rudyard Kipling's American wife who followed her husband to England when he lost his love for America, but she knew that she would feel too estranged in Morocco, she'd look too different, and would have to be too dependent on Lamin for everything. She was too independent to accept that lifestyle. She also knew that she had ran out of reasons to lure Lamin, make him stay, renew his faith in America; that he had thought about everything, turned every idea, every reason, upside down, looked at everything from every possible perspective, tried to imagine how it was when he first landed in New York, the exuberance, the feeling of being on top of the world, the waiters and waitresses in his favorite Greek diner, next to Sloane House, on 34th Street, watching the *Godfather* trilogy in a revival house for the price of one show in a regular theater, reading the reviews of Vincent Canby and looking for books in the main public library. And he thought about the wild days, too, his own dolce vita moments, when people really talked about art and the theater, before buses started offloading huge groups in Broadway and at the steps of the Metropolitan Museum of Art. That ink-stained America was gone forever; it took him with her, in directions unknown, making him feel as if were suspended over the Statue of Liberty, trying to decide which way his America left, and for how long.

"Let me provoke you a bit," I said, as the clock approached noon. "Was it—she—ever there? America."

"Yes, she was. Like a factory is in the industrial zone, a warehouse just next to it, and a hotel is down the road. What I didn't realize is that you go there to work, make money, not to live the way we do here, there in Spain, over there in France or Italy. There was freedom, too. To collect the cash and ride into the sunset, or marry a luscious blonde and live in California. Come back wearing green pants and chewing gum. It was the land of fables. It still is, but there is no fun now, at least not for me. In any case, my soil has called me back. Just like that. It had been whispering in my ears for decades, years; it grew strident in its persistence. I couldn't ignore it any longer."

I couldn't help but think about the timing, Europeans rising up to hold on to their heritage, their memories, to fight bureaucrats who lived by paper and numbers, not bread, wine, and cheese, olive trees, or real soccer, and I wondered whether Donald Trump and had anything to do with his decision to leave, walk away from more than thirty-five years, from his work, so I asked him.

"You kiddin'? Of course not. I never cared about the two-party system or mainstream political squabbles. I am more interested in how Americans work out their differences, manage their neuroses. Frightening, really. To me, Trump is the embodiment of an America—the country of deplorables—that self-righteous elites can't tolerate. A culture where Blondie chased bounties and Tuco stole cash. America is now mostly populated by a race of lonely, disoriented, medicated, and angry angels. Latter-day saints, believing that their pristine city upon the hill—wait, what am I saying?—thinking that their fenced houses in the suburbs, mansions in California, and duplexes in Manhattan are the ultimate expression of civilized life, which the Donald is tarnishing with his gold-and-marble interiors, unpresidential tweets and infantile utterances. There is an honesty about the Trump phenomenon that is provocative. Reminds me of Las Vegas. Excesses and mirages. Remember, America is a nation of hustlers, not a society of well-bred bourgeois types. Forget the aristocracy—that is profoundly anti-

American. Jesse Ventura is another version of this American spirit--the homo *americanus* genius personified."

"I was going to say that people—at least those who know you—would be confused by this thinking. Weren't you a Marxist?"

"Still am, in some fundamental ways. For purposes of cultural criticism which, to me, includes social relations. There is so much ignorance now about Marx that his thinking has been reduced to socialism versus capitalism."

"But why Trump and Ventura? Their populism? Courage to defy the righteous mob?"

"Partly, but also more. I am not sure how you've experienced your time in America. For me, in some sense, it is a movie that I have never stopped watching. The American drama is what always has fascinated me. The conquest of the new world and the power struggles that define the fate of an uprooted people. The insecurity that gnaws at every American. That hidden look of deep anxiety on every face. I live among my colleagues more like an anthropologist than a member of society."

"Sociologist?"

"No, anthropologist. Socially speaking, the States is more primitive than most underdeveloped nations in the world."

"So, you don't see the laissez-faire optimism that you liked so much, the promise you wrote about?"

"Oh, it's still there, and I am actually excited by this new progressive wave—free education, free health care— but I can't wait much longer for the promised land. My ancestral one has a more powerful claim now. Don't forget, too, we are very lucky. I am not back in some failed state. I am in Morocco, Tangier. The only place where I can be fully myself."

"Not even Spain? Teresa?"

"Not even. They will remain the dream. Not just mine, but Morocco's as well. Not France. Too emotionally distant from us. That corrosive cynicism, the depressing tone, and the lifelessness of it all. This is not to say I don't worry about Spain also. There is a coldness, like a mist, that is slowly descending on that country. Maybe it's the effect of the Euopean Union, northern ways that are dampening the land. But here, here, here's where my soul rests. The sea that separates us is a good thing."

Lamin looked away again as my imagination took me back to New Jersey, to the university where he had spent his entire academic career, watching a sort of rustic place, already out of date in the 1990s, where he found comfort in the company of Jake and other scholars from another age, who published books and argued about ideas in public, first using Xerox machines and mailboxes—real mailboxes—before migrating, as we now say, to email, with the same exchanges reaching every mailbox in the university, and he, Lamin, would get reproaches from busy employees, complaining that his opinions were wasting their time because they, these employees, had to go through the arduous process of pressing the delete button. He thought he could speak in faculty meetings, but every time he tried to voice an opinion he was shut down for violating Robert's Rules of Order, time and time again until he decided to find out who this speech codifier was. A military engineer from the nineteenth century, it turned out. I saw Lamin running home to Jen exclaiming: "Makes perfect sense. We are free to speak here only if we follow a military code." And Jen would try to make the best of the situation, but he would be gone, with his three or four colleagues who had become pariahs *in situ*, three men and one woman who had found themselves working not in a university but in a savings bank, where the talk was about full-time equivalents, revenue, budgets, discounts, accounts, and identity theft. A new caste of administrator started showing up talking about student outcomes, innovation, and a learning process that made the student master of his or her education, with the professor reduced to the role of facilitator, while consultants, with radiant smiles, would say how good that was. Before long, Lamin started hearing that education on the Internet or maybe one that was just hybrid, half online and half in the classroom, was the future. Then he was ordered to read books about leadership for retreats that were aimed at showing professors how to work together as a team, as if they were in an assembly line, not designed by a life of reading and contemplation to be fiercely autonomous, solitary, unbowed by the dictates of the masses, with only one mission: to preserve knowledge and share it as best as one could. He longed for the days when Professor Getzel would ask for a cigarette in class and light it up, savoring the smoke along with a literary turn of phrase, an anecdotal story about Ralph Ellison, and the students sitting there in awe, not as masters of the classroom, but as grateful disciples of a man who wrote the book on American literature. He remembered the night he had to find an underground bar in Manhattan where his professors and fellow graduate students had organized a reading that began at 10 pm and the poetry professor who always walked the hallways of the university in a fog, with a visible hangover, suddenly appeared on stage, fully awake, to read a poem about the monologue of a third-rate musician in a bar in Manhattan at three in the morning, a fifty-five-year-old man trying to map out his life while accompanying a cabaret singer with the voice of a drill sergeant, without the trace of a feminine note in it. He wondered whether that professor was still alive, if he had survived the regime changes that washed over the land since the 1980s, the coming of the health and wellness police, and the rise of the threat industry. His students started telling him that his reading assignments and discussions in class gave them headaches before they stopped reading books altogether. People wanted soundbites, Ted talks, and podcasts. They wanted to surf, not dive; browse, not read; sample, not eat. By this time, his three or four colleagues had all died. He was left alone in this new order, yet another poignant reminder that he had cashed in his American chips and was now facing the void of the future alone.

"Like you, I had gone to the States to study, to discover this mesmerizing country, to know its literature and history, and I enjoyed every minute of my student days. We had high hopes for the humanities because we believed that no self-respecting politician or businessman could ever go against it, but it was the blind forces of the market that have decided that there is no money in art or philosophy. Universities have turned into training centers to justify the astronomical cost shouldered by the students. To have students borrow tens of thousands of dollars to pay for their education can only happen in a society that despises its youth and higher learning."

The tsunami of change that had engulfed his mythical America left him breathless. For Lamin, America was an adopted nation; he chose it because it promised new horizons and opportunities; it allowed him to expand and grow, meet new people and races; it may even have been the antidote to the traditions that had stifled his native land. He had been too enchanted to see the cracks, the flaws, too awed to feel the coldness of its love, witness the misery of its people, their poverty in their wealth, and their utter wretchedness in their poverty. His America had become terribly dehumanized, with people glued to their screens and starved for the basic human touch.

"To be with flesh-and-blood humans," Lamin said, "is now a luxury. Robots and avatars are the new companions."

I asked if its old age causing this, his empty nest, the Nordic love of his wife, the constant sight of manicured lawns and rows of well-appointed houses, the absence of cafes with waiters, the death of live customer service people, and the obsolescence of the American-born worker to the point that the New York Mafia has to feed its ranks from Italy. Yes, he answered. In the years leading up to his return, he kept listening over and over again to the four Highwaymen reminding him of his America, the one he discovered in the cinemas of Tangier— Maghreb, Alacazar, Capitol, and American—all these theaters that have ceased to exist, as if they had been rendered useless with the changing of times, with the death of old heroes and the changing mores. The only question that remained was how to disentangle himself from the life he had built in America.

"I had spent many years thinking about that, trying to find a rational way to do it. In the end, I realized that returning to your native land is the same as immigrating to a new one—it requires courage, throwing caution to the wind, willingness to be a misfit, enduring the frustrations of the newcomer, living with a thousand, a million regrets. I turned things over and over again in my head, but the more I did, the more I was subjected to that paralyzing voice of reason, cautioning me to think about this, this and that, things like compound interest in my retirement account, health insurance, and the family.

And I've got to confess, I listened to that voice for too long, pretending to be the responsible grown up, you know, someone who thinks about money and security, but I didn't dare take my salvation seriously. Salvation. And as in my first days in America, it was literature and art that came to my rescue."

"How so? For most people it's religion, I imagine. The fear of death."

"That's absolutely not me, Rafik. Religion has never inspired courage in me. It leads to surrender. It is, in fact, anti-human."

"But so many acts of bravery, as well as violence, I must admit, are motivated by religion."

"I get that, but it's like having the insurance you will be paid off, rewarded for whatever deeds you have committed according to some scriptural rule. Not so with art and literature. It's the human facing his own self without mediation, confronting the cosmos, absent and indifferent, and still extracting meaning from it, making it beautiful, worth being a part of, until you can longer do so. That, to me, is real courage. Artists are the real heroes of our civilization. Life without them is not worth living. Imagine that!"

And that's how it was with Lamin. In a few words, he managed to upend everything in my head, make me question my own assumptions, push me to examine myself more rigorously, and think again about my future, as our conversation was gradually coming to an end. Just as he had developed an idea of America through movies, his escape was prompted by accidental readings, books like Stephen Greenblatt's *The Swerve* telling the story of the book hunter Possio Bracciolini who in 1417 discovered a lost copy of the poem *On the Nature of Things* and introduced the long-forgotten philosophy of Epicurus to the world. Lamin beheld a man who had risen to the top of the Italian social hierarchy and lost it all, but he remained steadfastly attached to his humanist vocation, unearthing long forgotten manuscripts until he stumbled on one that would change the direction of history. Of course, Lamin read the poem by Lucretius, composed in the century before the birth of Jesus, as believers might read the Bible or the Quran. As he kept reading an eclectic collection of books, a consistent message kept emanating from their pages, despite the fact that they are separated by time, space and language. The gods of the humanities had encoded a simple message just for him, and the message was to run, run to suffer life, not fools, not zombies, and not the industrialized creatures that roam the pathways of our high-tech environments.

I wanted to know how, exactly, he made his exit.

"It happened not long after I returned from Morocco following my mother's death. As you know, the only person I had left in Madison was Jen—sweet Jen. She did a good job keeping in touch with Yussef at his university, teaching and chairing her department. She was getting increasingly interested in administration—she was very good at it—perhaps as a way to keep herself busy in case I left. It was an odd situation—we were sort of mourning our impending separation not because we were fighting or we fell out of love (one of the most cowardly excuses for divorce), but because I was, like some kind of misplaced plant, shriveling and getting increasingly asphyxiated in Madison. We didn't know how to feel or how to express our feelings. I kept thinking of Poe, for some reason. Sometimes, we'd surprise ourselves by erupting in laughter; other times, we'd just take off for the city and indulge in every possible treat we could find. Then it was back to the routine, my office, the meetings, the endless discussions about identity, what other tradition will innovators disrupt, what new species will they invent, how to feel or think about the world, which scandal is worth discussing around the clock, who is going to win the next election, and the next, and then the next one, and on and on."

He paused for a second, then asked:

"Have you seen the film *L'auberge Espagnole*?"

"No. What is it about?"

"It's a movie about university students from different European countries sharing an apartment in Barcelona. You definitely must watch it. The main protagonist is a young French man your age. After a wild experience, including an affair with the wife of a doctor who hosts him, he returns to Paris to start a job in a formal corporate government office. He runs away before the end of the day. He just can't make it. He chooses a life of writing instead."

Why was Lamin saying this? Was he talking about what he decided to do, after more than thirty five years of living the pretense, the dream? Was he talking about me, the son of his friend who has chosen to live out what my father couldn't do, due to his sense of responsibility? Or was he talking about us both, literary types, out of place in the age of duty-free deals? I was about to drift with more speculations, when I realized that I had to keep myself together for this final encounter

"I will definitely check it out. Sounds like a good film."

"You are already ahead. You have all the time in the word to arrange your life, rearrange it, and live bravely, heroically, whether here in Morocco, the States, or some other place."

"If I may, Si Lamin, you didn't do badly yourself. You took a huge risk when you left for New York. You were alone."

"Yes, I was, and that made all the difference. Love, families, jobs, and reputations had turned me into a coward until that day when I walked out of my office in the university. I didn't announce anything to anyone. Just walked away and never returned. If I had done anything else, I would have betrayed myself, so I let myself speak, my body move, and mind fly. There is nothing like the thrill of walking away from the tyranny of banality. The rest was easy after that. I went home and told Jen that I was leaving in three days. By the end of March, I was here."

I finally understood what my father meant when he said that entering a hammam is not the same as leaving it. I thought of the older Jewish lady I had known in New York, one I had seen almost every time I went to my favorite diner, until one day she walked in looking utterly different, a much skinnier version of herself, much younger from afar, yet somewhat visibly older up close, an expression in bone and flesh of the somewhat disturbing paradoxical effect of people when they lose a lot of weight, the fat that melts away, leaving them utterly naked, weak, brittle, not at all the young and vibrant body they had imagined and dreamed of displaying. I complimented her, asking her how she managed to lose so much weight. She replied, "Nothing to it, honey, because I was losing it all the time you have known me, it was a long process, but it was slow, so you didn't notice. Until now. It took a long time for me to get fat; it happened slowly, imperceptibly, until one day I realized I was an old fat lady. I wasn't happy—let's it put this way—not depressed, just not happy, so I started a process of reversal, undoing what I had accumulated, what happened to my body, during all the time I was raising children, working, and taking care of a busy husband. The children are gone now, the husband dead, I am retired, but I was left with my body, a memory of labor in flesh. I decided to let go of it, too, and see where I would end up."

I knew that giving up an entire life, with a wife and child, a professor's job and whatever rare genuine friends he had been able to make in those thirty-five-plus years, was not going to be easy. Lamin was returning to his city, for sure, but it was also a developing nation in a state of limbo, not knowing what path it would take. I worried (I must admit), as I looked at his face in the early afternoon light, whether his scholarly mind (if that's the word) would end up being scattered away by the fierce *sharqi* winds, melting under the steady Mediterranean sun, a tragedy, a tragedy. Maybe it was my age that provoked these impressions, a bit too young to get that he was still in his prime, far from being done, that he was ready for another full life, not a life of nostalgia, but of work. What kind of work was the question.

I remembered what my father had told me, the conversations they had over the last ten years, including those they had just before my arrival, as they huddled in quiet hotel restaurants, in my father's office in Rabat, in the Cafe de Paris in Tangier, two men who had grown up together in the same neighborhood and saw one another go in different directions, one to build the infrastructure of Morocco, laying out hundreds of miles of tracks to connect people across the land, moving them faster than any other train in Africa could, managing thousands of workers, and working twenty-four hours a day, quite literally, to keep an eye on the smooth running on an impossible operation, all to catapult Morocco to higher ranks, allow Moroccans to feel good about their country, themselves, and my father fielding, bravely, the thousand arrows shot at him from every direction, including from sneaky dishonest Islamists, who cared nothing about their nation, and only dreamt of a pie-in-the-sky caliphate that had nothing to do with our people, yes, us, not knowing that my father is a *hajj*, my family deeply steeped in the Islamic tradition, real Islam, the spiritual variety, Jesus's true philosophy, take care of your soul and leave the corrupting stuff to politicians, the power-hungry, the money-makers, the ostentatious types, seekers of luxury products, fancy vacations, the real housewives of Casablanca, Rabat, Marrakech, name droppers with Swiss bank accounts and real estate in fancy European cities, and my father who cared nothing about them, choosing instead to argue month after month, year after year, with his friend Lamin about what is best for the country, and Lamin insisting that no decency is possible without allowing people to choose their beliefs, find their own clues to their fulfillment because, as Lamin insisted again and again, he cares nothing about freedom because there is no absolute freedom, we are all constrained by something, we've got to serve somebody, as Bob Dylan put it, or something, like nature, biology, and the random violence in the streets. Lamin wanted to build a spaceship to unfettered imagination, nurture poetic sensibilities in people subjected to the unremitting cruelties of our kitschy civilization and unlock Morocco's box of marvels to unleash a trillion acts of magic. And my engineer father, instead of finding his literary friend's project to be hopelessly quixotic, took it with utter seriousness, knowing full well that it is the spirit that moves the world, that his trains take people places but only the spirit can really move them. The old friends were proof to anyone who listened that poetry and technology were part of the same order of things since life without them would be long and arduous. This was not a war of cultures but a communion of spirits.

I pictured the two men walking back to their old neighborhood of Columbia in Msallah, sitting on the same doorstep of Cojo's house, watching the square absentmindedly as they had done many decades before, looking at everything and nothing, thinking of the days when they played soccer in those streets, got in trouble with the grocer for hitting his merchandise and wares, being chased away by the *farran* owner, the man who lived and slept in his underground store and only knew the world through the endless wooden trays of dough entrusted to him to be baked to perfection, and my father and Lamin just sat there, occasionally acknowledging a passerby, an old friend, somebody's mother, or getting up to let the house's tenants get out or walk in.

"Feels like I have taken a round trip on the Al Boraq," Lamin teased his friend by referring to the new high-speed train he had launched. "Not enough time to fall asleep or to reach the seven heavens."

"It does—doesn't it?" acknowledged my father.

And after an hour or so, they got up and walked away, my father to visit his parents, and Lamin in the direction of Cinema Lux, which had become a small mall.

When my father told me about this episode, I thought of theories of language and communication that I had read, how the newly met never stop talking, speaking furiously to connect, while old friends, couples, don't need to say a word, they just sit there, speak silently, letting their memories roam. The two friends had reached this blessed spot, they had this luxury of knowing each other for almost six decades, living through gains and losses, and arriving safely at their starting point. I knew, at that moment, that I would never be part of Lamin's world, I, the son of the best father, growing up in total comfort, best house, best neighborhood, great education, good health, but no Columbia friends, no enduring friendships, all digital, like a musical video spot, a Pepsi ad, Banana Republic, safari trips to nowhere, no real substance, not even heartbreaking love. We just like and dislike each other with abandon.

Around two in the afternoon, Lamin got up and said it was time to have lunch. I insisted on paying the bill, but he said he'd have none of that. He wanted to have a real Moroccan meal and invited me to join him at one of the nondescript restaurants just one block behind his apartment building. We were attended to the moment we sat down and our order of white beans, grilled sardines, and lentils was delivered within five minutes. The place was teeming with people, waiters rushing back and forth, customers talking animatedly, and yet there was no hubbub, only a joyful lunchtime experience, reminding us that a good life in Tangier was available to anyone who can afford twenty dirhams.

After lunch, we walked a couple of short blocks to Cafe La Colombe for a cup of coffee. As we sat facing the Le Boulevard, Lamin asked if I had learned anything so far from his experience. It was a good question that I wasn't sure how to answer. I kept looking out the large windows hoping to be inspired, to find the right words, to know—if anything can be known—what it was exactly I was doing by talking to Lamin. I had a moment of relief when the waiter wiped our table and delivered our two cups of black coffee—a *café allongé* for me and a double espresso for him—and two small bottles of water. Lamin took a sip and, probably sensing my discomfort at not finding a quick answer, hastened to speak first, reassure me:

"I can't answer that question myself," he said. "I don't know what I learned from own life. It is too mundane, too small to amount to anything. I haven't done anything to change my environment, change the world, make a difference, as the Americans never cease to repeat. I never believed in the cult of legacies, doing something that outlasts you, that would make people remember you. That's the Pharaoh complex, the desperate quest for immortality, to the point of going to one's grave mummified and surrounded by artifacts, waiting for the day of resurrection, ready to resume life again. To me, living in the here and now is everything we've got. Paradise is whatever gives us joy, be it a book, park, bar, country, language, friend, woman, whatever. There is no posterity for me, except for whatever I transmitted genetically. Yussef. His children, maybe. I didn't write to survive my physical death but to live my emotions fully in this world. The only difference you can make is in yourself, and it is not a difference but a confirmation, an acknowledgment of yourself, for the self is born complete, as is, in no need of alteration, only recovery if it gets lost, damaged, mutilated by a never-ending conspiracy of confusion, ambiguity that mushrooms into clouds of darkness, leaving you, me, stranded, unable to see through the fog, lost on your feet. In that sense, all lives are dramas, even epic ones, unfolding quietly in endless ways, in the shadows because—haven't you ever considered this?—a person is a walking battlefield, pulled in all directions, his mind racing ahead to make sense of his condition, his future, his safety, and you know it— don't you, Rafik?—that this is a process without end, it will go on and on, until, as we say, Allah inherits the earth and what's on it."

"No, Si Lamin, there is more to your story," I dared reply boldly, without hesitation. "There is something that has attracted me to your life. It's not dramatic by the standards of our fake news—I'll grant you that. But, no, it is interesting enough that it made a difference to me, I postponed my doctoral studies, for God's sake, and left the United States to write about you. I have talked to many people and will continue to do so until I get your story right, or somewhat right. I am trying to find the right words, approach, the proper *cadre*, as they say here in French, to tell it. As an aspiring writer, Si Lamin, I don't necessarily find traditional heroes interesting—the kinds who lead wars, start companies, climb impossible mountains, or break records. But your life, yes, it speaks to me. Why? That's the question. Why?"

Lamin took another sip from his espresso and looked at me, as if scrutinizing my face for messages.

"You are on to something, Rafik. It is the interior life that matters to you most, and that includes the life of the mind, agonizing decisions informed by a whole education—parents, neighborhoods, society, religion, and, for us, ideas. Maybe you see your future in me and don't like some aspects of it. I got to give you credit for acting as fast as you did, before you entangle your life in America, France, the West, whatever, and have to make these big decisions, extricate yourself from decades of commitments, thick layers of accumulated stuff, the American way, you know, the dream."

"I would have agreed, Si Lamin, if I thought I had depth and foresight to think like that. I do have a certain courage—the courage to give up my studies to write about you, but I also have the assurances of my father, my family. It's not victory or death, as may have been somewhat the case in your time. I mean you had nothing, after you spent a year in New York, to come back to. You had given up all opportunities for America. Your arrival in 1983 was nothing like mine in 2017. I had visited before as a tourist; I came with my father to Disney in Florida when I was in elementary school; I visited New York and Boston on my own, when I was in France. You may have been a student when you arrived, but there was a feeling of no return at that time, the die was cast, you had no option but to succeed. Whether you like it or not, you discovered America as an immigrant-student; I discovered it first as a tourist, a shopper, a consumer of American, global entertainment. I was spending money in America; America gave you money. This, alone, makes my relationship to America, travel, being away, less traumatic, easy, even banal."

Lamin looked somewhat stunned. His eyes, sharp and alive, nestled in a facial expression that reminded me of mummies reposing serenely in some dark chamber in the desert, lit up and danced with delight. I had never seen an expression like that before, one that you had to be very close to see, feel; it almost wasn't natural, human. He moved his face slightly to the right, as if he were now communing with other forces, those who had just visited him from some other realm, while I, the tourist, the shopper, the son of his friend, just sat there as exhibit A, a specimen of a world that was no longer his. The whole thing was utterly confusing to me. Just when I thought I had reached him with my ideas, thoughts, analysis; just when I finally managed to awaken him to my presence; just when we were about to shake hands for the first time—I mean really shake hands—he started drifting away to god knows where. I looked at him, hoping to explain this unsettling mood by the fact that he had grown old, that Lamin was happy to have found an accomplice in me, but that was not it. Not at all. In fact, Lamin looked younger than ever—vibrant, healthy, bursting with energy, so out of place in a busy city famous for its slow rhythms. Nothing could contain him at that moment. He was out of reach. He was gone. What had I done?

My confusion was turning into frustration. At this moment, I felt that he was not being fair to me in his sudden state of nirvana. These were supposed to be solemn moments of reflection and farewells, not silent acts of ecstasy. The glitter in Lamin's eyes derailed my narrative, my story, just when I was about to wrap up my meeting with him. What was he thinking, feeling, knowing? What?

"What you just said, Rafik, what you said. America was America when there was an Ellis Island, a statue welcoming the huddled masses, the wretched of the earth, those who wanted to make a living, a place to live, food on the table, jobs to be had. You are right: Coming to America for me was a huge deal. It felt like I was headed to a different planet when I landed. There was this feeling of opportunity, a second chance, maybe even a third one. It no longer has the same meaning. The innovators in Silicon Valley and Hollywood have managed to turn their country into a banal brand, even a grotesque experience, changing their society app by app, one identity after another, a country of bounty hunters, lawyers seeking damages, overmedicated people unable to cope with stress, a nation of orphans, emotional orphans, unfed people, no real emotions, no touch, no real kindness, these people—not sure if you had the time to see them in New York because the pace is too busy— are now taking their revenge on each other. It is—it is—a vast battleground. Bloody. A war waged by clean, well-shaved, health-conscious people to make the world in their own image—happy, basking in the cold freedom of democracy, keeping track of their rights, and lost in the apocalyptic cycles of consumption. Pity the stranger in this land."

Pity the stranger!

I insisted on paying the bill this time. We stood for a few moments motionless on the sidewalk not knowing what to do next. I was headed to Rabat to be with my family and my train was leaving in forty-five minutes. I assumed Lamin was trying to figure out where to go next at four in the afternoon. All of a sudden, he snapped out of his brief reverie, looked me straight into the eye, extended a hand and pulled me toward him in a big, gentle hug.

"Write your feelings, Rafik, and don't worry about the rest. There is nothing else."

I promised I would. I walked down Le Boulevard all the way to the train station and boarded the Al Boraq to Rabat. As the unfinished landscape zipped past me, I kept struggling with the glitter in Lamin's eye. It was of an intensity and a kind I had never seen before; there was something otherworldly about it. At that moment in Cafe La Colombe he may have received the answer that banishes all doubt and had the unshakeable confirmation that he had made the right decision. But what was he going to do? He had already made peace with the ghosts of his past, stood silently in front of apartment buildings erected on the spot that used to be Bukhash-khash, the clinic where he was born, the graves where his parents were buried, and the schools where he studied. He had already walked the streets of Msallah, Medina and Marshan daily, in a never-ending loop, determined to unearth buried memories. He spent many evenings talking about Aziz to La Batul in her house in Souani, getting out exhausted each time and heading directly to Le Pain Nu for drinks. He even traveled to Fez to imagine what might have been had he not chosen to go to New York.

By the time the train arrived at the Agdal station in Rabat, I realized I was asking the wrong question. Lamin didn't return to Tangier with a big plan for the future, but as a man seeking a second chance in his own native land. He had enough memories and imagination to keep him busy for five or six lifetimes. The problem was mine, really. What was I going to do, now that I have finished writing my book?